winter
of grace

# KATE CONSTABLE

ALLEN&UNWIN

This edition published in 2011
First published in 2009

Allen & Unwin
83 Alexander Street
Crows Nest NSW 2065
Australia
*Phone*   (61 2) 8425 0100
*Fax*     (61 2) 9906 2218
*Email*   info@allenandunwin.com
*Web*     www.allenandunwin.com

ISBN 978 1 74237 772 8

Design based on cover design by Tabitha King and Bruno Herfst
Cover photo: PhotoAlto/Laurence Mouton © 2008 Jupiterimages Corporation
Text design by Bruno Herfst
Set in 12.5/15 pt Fournier by Midland Typesetters, Australia
Printed in China at Everbest Printing Co.

10 9 8 7 6 5 4 3 2 1

THE BUS WAS packed, but more and more people kept piling on: mothers with strollers, old people in cardigans, dads with babies strapped to their chests, women in suits, boys in caps. The atmosphere was buzzing.

'It must have been like this in World War II.' I had to twist sideways to yell into Stella's ear. 'When the pilots went off on their bombing raids. All in it together, with a mission, with a purpose.'

Stella rolled her eyes. 'Yeah, Bridie, except this is a peace rally. We're trying to *stop* soldiers going on bombing raids? That's the whole point?'

'Oh, yeah. Bad example.' I flushed; no one could make me feel like an idiot quicker than Stella. But then she grinned and squeezed my arm, and I remembered that no one else could cheer me up as fast, either.

'This is going to be *so good*!' She shook her silvery hair off her face, and her pale blue eyes shone with excitement. It nearly made me choke up, I missed her so much.

Stella and I have been best friends since Year 7, but at the end of last year her parents decided to send her to St Margaret's for Year 11 and 12. St Margaret's is a private Catholic school. Stella's family are kind of Catholic; at least, Nana Kincaid is. Stella's dad, Paul, stopped going to church years ago but he must still be slightly Catholic deep down, because he does loads of volunteer work for church charities and, according to Stella, he thought St Margaret's would 'expose her to some moral structure'. Mish, Stella's mum, was never Catholic. She isn't anything, like me and Mum. But she said St Marg's was a good school and it wouldn't do Stella any harm – not in two years, anyway.

Stella didn't agree. She'd decided to hate it.

'Is anyone from your school coming?' I asked her.

Stella rolled her eyes again. 'Are you kidding? They never do *anything* political. I had to tell them who the Dalai Lama was. Do you know what they've started calling me? PMK. Prime Minister Kincaid. *Seriously.*' Stella snorted, but I could see she was proud of it.

I twisted back and gazed out of the bus window at the bright winter day, at the cars and shops and hurrying crowds. It wasn't surprising that Stella had already established herself at her new school after only a term and a half. Mish always says she is a forceful personality. And I was glad – for her – that she'd settled in so fast. But all year I'd been wandering round our old school, feeling as if I'd had a limb amputated. We still saw each other, because she lived just down the road, but it wasn't the same.

Stella must have guessed what I was thinking, because she

nudged me with her elbow and said, 'St Marg's is full of giggling morons. All they ever talk about is clothes and lipstick; they don't care about anything *important*. There's no one there like *you*.'

That was the great thing about Stella; she always knew how to make me feel special, singled out in the spotlight of her attention. Without her, I felt as if no one noticed me. Even Mum was always too busy with work now to have much time for me.

But then Stella added, 'Plus they're all girls, obviously.' Another eye roll. 'Bor-ing.'

I suspected that one reason Paul and Mish wanted Stella to switch schools was so that she wouldn't be distracted by boys. As if *that* was going to work. 'So who do you hang out with?'

'Oh, no one much,' said Stella vaguely, as the bus lurched forward. 'This girl Clare – Maria Tommaso – no one, really.'

She *said* no one, but I knew Stella would never be without friends. I imagined her at lunchtime, lecturing the giggling morons on global politics, shaking her hair back and rolling her eyes at them. Not that I was completely friendless myself – I mean, I wasn't a total loser or anything. But Stella and I had done everything together, and now she was gone. Everyone else was still in their same groups, and I drifted around from one gang to another. I always had someone to sit with, someone to talk to. But it wasn't the same.

By now the bus was so crammed we could hardly breathe, and it crawled through the city at a snail's pace. When the driver opened the doors, we all spilled out onto the road, surging onto the footpath, swept up into the massive crowd that was flooding into the centre of the city. Almost at once I lost Stella in the push and shove of bodies, and I panicked until she reappeared beside me, breathless and beaming. 'Wow!' she yelled. 'This is *amazing*!'

The streets were choked with people, a river of marchers flowing into the sea of people gathered in the park. It was a swelling ocean of peaceful protesters, the biggest crowd I'd ever seen. A guy beside us with swinging dreadlocks yelled into his phone, 'Two hundred thousand! I said, *two hundred thousand*!'

Stella and I grinned at each other. That was two full MCGs, a double Grand Final, and we were part of it! We linked arms and plunged into the throng, chanting at the tops of our voices.

*One two three four, we don't want another war! Five six seven eight, stop the killing, stop the hate!*

A group behind us tried to start a chorus of 'All we are saying, is give peace a chance,' but they couldn't compete with our mighty one-two-three-four. We stamped and chanted and whooped and cheered – a surging tide of people. Banners waved and placards bobbed all around us, all kinds of groups and clubs and communities, some I'd never even heard of: Rotarians and socialists, greenies and church groups, Asian students and Italian soccer clubs, Muslims for Peace, West Hill Buddhists, Jews Against War, Uniting Church Says No More Missiles, Quaker Prayer for Peace Vigil. People from every suburb and all over the state were jumbled together to make a massive *peace-beast* that roared and swelled along the city streets.

We were mightier than politicians and dictators, mightier than an army, and Stella and I were part of it, lifted up and buoyed along, joyous and powerful, all of us united. We'd taken over the streets, forced out the traffic. For the next few hours, *we* owned the road. It felt like we owned the whole world.

And people looked at each other, really looked each other in the eye and smiled. I'd never realised how rare that is. Usually in crowds, I kept my head down; I didn't look at people properly. They were just anonymous bodies blocking my path, and I guess I was the same to them.

But today was different. We were all shouting together, all swept up in the same huge emotion, the same huge purpose. Stella and I chanted till our throats were raw, but our voices were lost, drowned in the communal roar. It was *awesome*.

That was the best part. After we reached the park, the marching and the chanting ground to a halt, and we all stood round and fidgeted, waiting for something else to happen. The speeches began, but we couldn't hear. There was a muffled sound of passionate voices, and whines from the microphones, and then wild cheers – obviously some people could hear all right – but Stella and I couldn't.

'This is pointless,' said Stella. 'Let's go.'

'We can't *go*!'

'Sure we can. There're two hundred thousand people here, think anyone's going to notice if we leave?'

I hesitated. Even if no one was watching, it still felt wrong to sneak away. But Stella was restless, so we squeezed through the crowd, *sorry, excuse me*, for what seemed like hours, until at last we popped out at the edge of the rally, right up at the top of the hill.

'Wow,' said Stella again, gazing down at the clogged park and the streets with as much satisfaction as if she'd conjured up the whole teeming crowd herself. 'There's no *way* they can ignore this—'

'Ssh! Is that Zita Mariposa?'

The acoustics were heaps better now we were out of the crush, and Zita Mariposa's ethereal voice, fine and strong as a silver wire, soared up from the park.

'I love this song,' breathed Stella, and I blinked away tears. There was a heavy, wonderful ache in my heart. Suddenly everything seemed so pure and so clear: the beauty of the music, the power of ordinary people who cared about the world. Nothing was impossible, there didn't have to be wars, or hatred, or destruction; the world could be saved. It was so simple, so clear; all the answers were right here, within our grasp.

Stella grabbed my arm. 'What's going on there?'

There was a shout, footsteps pounded. I swung round and saw a blur of movement on the other side of the road. Three guys were racing along the footpath. One of them yelled, 'Get him!'

Further down the street a young guy with his arms up round his head was stumbling along like a wounded animal. They were gaining on him. One of the pursuers grabbed for his jacket, he tore himself free for a second – then he was down. In an instant they were on him, baying like a pack of wolves.

6

He disappeared into a flurry of punching piston elbows and kicking boots.

Stella screamed, '*Stop that*, you pigs!' and before I knew what was happening, she was sprinting across the road. She'd wrenched her phone from her pocket and she brandished it like a weapon. 'I'm filming you!' she shouted. 'You're going on YouTube!'

Feeling sick, I took off after her. A minute ago there had been police everywhere, now there wasn't a single uniform in sight. I shouted, 'Help! Help!', shrugged off my backpack and swung it by its straps in what I hoped was a threatening manner. It was just instinct. For all we knew, the young guy could have been a mugger and we were barging in on a citizens' arrest. And if he wasn't – they were three big burly thugs. We were two sixteen-year-old girls. What were we going to do, poke them in the stomach with Stella's mobile phone?

All this flashed through my head in the half-second it took to cross the road. One of the guys looked round when he heard Stella screaming, and luckily for us, he grabbed his mates and they all took off down a laneway as if tigers were after them.

Which left me and Stella. And a half-dead guy lying on the footpath.

THE ATTACKERS HAD already vanished round a corner, but Stella shrieked after them, 'I've got you on video, suckers!' She took a deeper breath. 'My dad's a policeman!'

'*Stella!*' Paul isn't a policeman; he works for an insurance company.

The poor boy was curled on the ground like a dead slater. I dropped down beside him and said stupidly, 'Are you okay?'

Clearly he was a long way from okay; but he moaned and stirred and unscrunched himself. I put my arm under him and helped him sit up.

'Oh my God,' I said. They must have kicked him in the eye, because blood was pouring down his face and his eye was completely swollen.

Stella knelt beside us. 'There must be St John's Ambulance people somewhere; they're always at big events.'

I stared around frantically but I couldn't see anyone useful, no first aid people and still no police. A couple of people stared at us as they walked past, but no one stopped to help, and most people pretended they couldn't see us. So much for all that global love and understanding.

8

'I'm fine,' said the boy faintly.

'No, you're not,' said Stella. She looked at me. 'Have you got anything to put on his eye?'

'Um …' I fished around helplessly in my backpack and then I remembered I had a couple of emergency sanitary pads. Could anything be more embarrassing? But this was definitely an emergency. Besides, what was worse, bleeding to death or holding a pad to your face?

'Here …' I hoped that in his dazed state he wouldn't notice what I'd handed him, and he didn't seem to. He pressed the pad to his eye and winced. But Stella noticed.

'Is that all you've got?' she hissed.

I grimaced at her. 'It's sterile and it soaks up blood. It's perfect.' In fact I could dimly remember a first-aid class at school where they'd told us exactly this; of course everyone had groaned *eew*, but who knew it would actually be useful in real life?

'We'll have to take him to hospital,' said Stella. 'It's only a few blocks. Can you walk?' she asked the boy. He was about our age, with a mop of thick tawny hair, and a dusting of freckles. The non-swollen eye seemed to be green-gold, presumably they both were. It was hard to tell, what with all the blood and scrapes and swelling bruises, but I thought he might be quite good-looking.

'I think I can,' he said, like the little engine, and obediently unfolded himself from the footpath, revealing himself to be about seven feet tall – well, pretty tall, anyway, in that gangly teenage boy way. Stella and I rushed to wedge ourselves under his armpits to stop him toppling over again.

'It's not far,' said Stella encouragingly.

'Okay,' the boy said faintly, and we began to half-lead, half-carry him along the street toward the hospital. He was heavy.

'What's your name?' panted Stella.

He had to think about it. 'Jay — Jay Ridley.' His voice was wobbly.

'I'm Stella Kincaid and this is Bridie Vandenberg.'

'Hi.' After a minute he added, 'Thanks.'

I said, 'Is there anyone you want to call?'

There was a long pause, then he said, 'My brother, Elliot ... He's at uni.'

'Wait ... till we get ... to the hospital,' panted Stella.

We didn't talk any more after that. Jay pressed the pad to his face but the blood still seeped out between his fingers, and every time his foot struck the footpath he let out a faint involuntary groan.

'We should have called an ambulance,' I said across Jay's back to Stella. 'We shouldn't have moved him. What if he's got internal injuries?'

'Who are you, Nurse Nancy?' growled Stella, so I knew she was worried too.

''S okay,' panted Jay valiantly. 'Nearly there.'

We managed to stagger along the last few hundred metres and as soon as we got inside the emergency department I'm ashamed to say we pretty much dropped him on the floor, he was just so heavy. Any further and I reckon one of us would have had a heart attack, not to mention a broken back.

Stella took charge, as usual. She was fabulous. As soon

as she'd caught her breath, she left me to guide Jay to a seat while she marched up and demanded immediate attention. The nurse on duty was a bit dismissive at first; they must get guys in there all the time, hurt in fights. But Stella insisted that he was an innocent bashing victim who needed urgent help, and surprisingly quickly they whisked him away and left us in the waiting room, unsure what to do next.

'We didn't call his brother,' said Stella.

'They'll probably do that, and we don't know his number,' I said. 'Maybe we should go.'

'We can't just *go*.' Stella echoed my words from half an hour before. 'Jay might want to say thanks. Anyway,' she thought of a much better reason, 'we're witnesses. The police will want to talk to us.'

'Oh, yeah, you're right.' We sat down in the waiting room, pleased to have a legitimate reason to hang around. I didn't get caught up in a real-life drama like this one every day, and I did genuinely want to see if Jay was all right. Stella – Stella just wanted Jay. I'd known her long enough to recognise the signs, and though she'd only just met him, it was clear she'd already developed a major crush. Who knows, if Stella hadn't got in first, I might have felt the same. It's pretty romantic to actually save a guy's life.

'Jay might feel weird about all this,' I warned Stella before she got too dreamy-eyed. 'Men have a lot of pride, you know. He might be embarrassed about being rescued by a girl.'

'Two girls,' said Stella.

'I didn't do anything. You're the one who scared them off.'

'You stuck his eyeball back in with a pad,' said Stella seriously, and this sent us both into a fit of giggles.

A nurse bustled out and gave us a disapproving look, which made us giggle even harder. 'You can see your friend now,' she said, and led us through the double doors and into a ward lined with beds with curtains round them. There was a strong smell of disinfectant.

Jay was sitting up in one of the beds with a huge bandage over his eye and round half his head, like an exaggerated cartoon victim. The sight of him did nothing to quench our giggles. But when he saw us, a happy, relieved smile spread over his face, and he reached out his hand. And funnily enough, that was what sobered us up; he was so glad we were there, it almost made me cry.

'Thanks so much,' he croaked. 'Thank you.'

Stella grabbed his hand and squeezed it – any excuse. 'Don't worry about it.' She plopped herself on the chair beside his bed as if she were already his girlfriend.

He gave her a dazed, dreamy grin, lopsided under the bandage. It occurred to me afterwards that he was probably drugged out on painkillers. 'Would you guys mind … would you be able to … could you stay till my brother gets here?'

'Of *course* we'll stay,' choked Stella.

'And the police are coming,' Jay added. He closed his good eye and leaned back on the pillows. Stella hung onto his hand and sighed with pleasure, and I looked round for another place to sit. There were no more chairs, so I perched on the end of the bed with my feet dangling. Jay drifted into sleep – either that or a coma – so we just sat there for ages, watching him. It was peaceful, though not very comfortable, and it was nice to feel that he needed us.

Eventually I remembered that I should call Mum, who was expecting us back. Since Stella was fully occupied with her hand-holding duties, and you're not allowed to use mobile phones in hospitals, I went outside to make the call.

It took forever to explain to Mum what was going on; she was much more concerned about what *might* have happened to me and Stella than what actually had happened to Jay.

'*Bridie!* It's all very well to play the Good Samaritan, but next time, just use your brains! They could have had knives; they could have raped you—'

'It was the middle of the city, Mum!'

'Being in the middle of the city didn't stop them beating up this poor boy, did it?' And of course there was no answer to that.

By the time I'd assured her that we were perfectly fine and got her off the phone and found my way back to Jay's bedside, he was awake again, and a police officer had arrived. Stella was showing him the footage from her phone. It wasn't very clear, but you could see them kicking into poor Jay on the ground. Jay looked a bit green as he watched it.

The officer took down my details and I told him what I'd seen, which didn't seem to be very helpful. I couldn't describe any of the guys, for instance; it had all happened too fast.

'Who were they, anyway?' said Stella. 'Why did they pick on Jay?' She squeezed his hand protectively.

The officer shrugged. 'You always get a few troublemakers at events like this. Stirs up tension, adrenalin rush, people get carried away. They see someone holding a placard and just lose it. Mob mentality takes over.'

'So they weren't muggers?' I said. 'You think it was political?' Talk about standing up for your beliefs: Jay had risked his life for the cause of peace. I almost envied him. Apart from the actual getting-hurt part.

The officer put away his notebook. 'Probably students, I'd say.'

'Students?' said Stella. 'Seriously?'

Stella can't wait to be a student; she's hanging out for uni. I'm not, so much. Mum's a lecturer and she's told me enough about her students for me to know they're not all glamorous and exciting.

'That's probably why they weren't too hard to scare off,' said the officer, which put a dent in our heroic pride. He stood up to go. 'If you remember anything else, here's my card,' he said to Jay. 'But I've got to be honest, mate; I don't think there's much chance of catching them.'

'Not even with my video?' Stella was disappointed.

'Not even with your video, love. Sorry.'

'Don't you want to keep my phone as evidence?'

The officer laughed. 'You'll need it more than we do. Wouldn't want to interfere with your social life.'

'Huh.' Stella gazed after him as he left. 'How lame is that? They're not even going to *try*.'

'It doesn't matter,' said Jay weakly. 'It was just a ... misunderstanding.'

'What, they misunderstood that your head wasn't a football?' I said.

But Jay was struggling upright, looking past me and Stella with an eager expression. 'My brother's here.'

Stella and I swivelled and saw another lanky young man striding toward us. He looked a lot like Jay, except his hair was cut shorter, and because he was a few years older, he'd filled out his frame and wasn't so gangly. But he had the same green-gold eyes and the same scattering of freckles across his nose. The main difference between the brothers was that instead of Jay's wide, glad smile, his face was screwed up in a scowl.

'This is Elliot,' said Jay happily, ignoring his brother's expression. 'Elliot, this is Bridie and Stella, they brought me to the hospital.'

'Thanks,' said Elliot curtly. 'No need to hold you up any longer.'

'That's okay,' said Stella. 'We don't have to be anywhere.' She was still sitting on the bedside chair, but at a glare from Elliot, she reluctantly stood up so he could take it. Elliot sat down, still scowling. Of course, he was probably just worried about his little brother, but he *looked* as if he was working himself up to kill somebody, and I didn't want it to be me.

'We'd better go,' I said hastily, sliding off the bed. 'Hope your eye's okay, Jay, hope you get better soon.'

'Wait! Can't I …' Jay looked at us shyly. With the bandage over his eye it was hard to tell if he was looking at both of us or one of us in particular. 'Can't I get your number? So I can thank you properly, when I'm not so …'

Feverishly, Stella rummaged for a scrap of paper.

'Elliot,' said Jay. 'Could you …?'

Elliot grimaced. He pulled a piece of pink paper from his bag and handed it to Stella, who scribbled her name and phone number. She wrote down mine too, because she is a fair person, really. Elliot refolded the paper and tucked it inside his coat. Then he turned the full power of his scowl onto us like a laser beam until we were forced to retreat out of the emergency ward and all the way back onto the street.

'The brother must do Law at uni,' said Stella. 'That pink paper was tutorial notepaper. I wonder why he wasn't at the rally, I bet all the other uni students were. Maybe he's pro-war.'

'Oh, no way. No one could be,' I said. 'He did seem pretty grumpy though.'

'He had no right to be,' said Stella. 'Not when we saved Jay's life.'

'You'd think he could have been a *tiny* bit grateful.'

'Who cares about the cranky brother?' Stella twirled on the footpath. 'I think I'm in love!'

'A good day's work then,' I said. 'We've stopped a war, saved a life and found you a boyfriend. Come on, let's get the train home.'

But I was thinking, *I bet we never hear from them again*, which made me slightly sad, because I liked Jay too, though not as much as Stella did. If he looked like his brother, under all that bruising, then he was definitely good-looking. I figured Elliot had thrown that pink paper straight in the bin.

But I was wrong.

I WAS WRONG ABOUT us stopping the war, too.

I heard the news on the radio first thing on Monday morning. It was like a punch to the stomach. But it wasn't a mistake; it was really happening. I sank down on the edge of my bed, feeling sick.

'Oh, God,' I said aloud. 'Oh, God.'

I sat there paralysed for a few more minutes, till I realised how late it was. I had to run.

Stella was already waiting out the front of her house, with Tim the dachshund twisting himself into a yappy knot round her ankles.

'Where've you *been*, I nearly left without you. Shut *up*, Tim!'

'Sorry.' I took over Tim's lead while Stella pulled on her gloves. 'Did you hear the news?'

'Nuh, what's happened?'

'The war – they've declared war. It's going ahead.'

Stella stopped in her tracks. 'Oh, no. You're kidding. But – how? People marched – all those people, all over the *world*. How can they just ignore that?'

'I don't know,' I said.

Stella scooped up Tim and pressed her face close to his smooth black coat; he wriggled round to give her nose a lick of comfort. 'How can this *happen*?' she said in a muffled voice.

'Why does anything bad happen? Why does a nice boy like Jay get beaten up? Why are people tortured, why do people kill each other, why are human beings so cruel and horrible?'

'It's God's will,' said Stella bitterly. 'That's what they'll say at school, I bet.' She sniffed fiercely. 'Stop wriggling, Timmy, I'll put you down when we get across the road.'

It was our turn to take Tim for a walk down by the river. There was a family roster: one morning it was Mish and Stella's little sister, Scarlet; the next it was Paul and her brother Tark; and every third morning it was Stella and me. We'd been doing it for three years, ever since Mish and Paul and Mum decided we were old enough to go out at dawn by ourselves. Of course, we had Tim to protect us, but since Tim's idea of protection was to jump at someone's knees and yap them to death, we didn't rely too much on him.

We sprinted across the highway with Stella carrying Tim; his little legs couldn't keep up. Safely on the other side, she set him down and he trotted off, his back half wagging. He knew the circuit: through the park, across the bridge and round past the boathouse, along the riverbank and back over the other bridge, then cut through the back streets and home by half-past seven to get ready for school. Normally I loved being up so early, while the world was all fresh and still, but there was nothing beautiful about today.

Since Stella had switched to St Marg's, our walks were practically the only time we got to see each other, and we always had heaps to discuss. But this morning I was too miserable to talk.

At last Stella said, 'Guess what?'

Now I could see she was bursting with news; she couldn't hang on a second longer. 'What?'

'He texted me! Last night, he texted me and asked for my address!'

It took me a moment to realise she was talking about Jay. 'Wow,' I said, trying to sound enthusiastic. I didn't want to spoil her excitement by telling her that he'd texted me too.

'What do you think it means? Do you think he'll just turn up on the doorstep? Tim, leave it … good boy.'

I bent to fondle Tim's ears. 'I don't think he'll be going anywhere just yet, with his eye all cut up.'

'Oh, yeah … of course. I keep forgetting he's wounded.'

I couldn't bring myself to get too worked up about Jay. All I could think about was the war; that a man in a suit had picked up a phone, and on the other side of the world other people, innocent people, were going to be blown apart. My stomach churned.

Stella said, 'Do you think I'm getting over-excited?'

'Hmm?' I made an effort. 'No … Jay's sweet.'

'The problem is, now I'm cut off from boys on a daily basis, I think I'm over-idealising them. Do you think that's dangerous?'

I smiled. 'Come back to school and look at Frankie and Will, that'll cure you.'

'I almost miss Frankie and Will, how tragic is that?' Stella was quiet for a minute. 'I hate St Marg's,' she said suddenly. 'I wish you were there.'

'Maybe I could swap too,' I said randomly, but as soon as the words were out of my mouth it seemed like a genius solution. Stella grabbed my arms and jumped up and down.

'Yes, yes! Why not? *Yes*!'

'Maybe we can't afford it,' I said doubtfully.

'Of course you can afford it, Lisa told me she just got a pay rise. You're loaded now.'

'We are?' Stella and my mum are great old mates; Mish and I get on really well, too. It's weird; sometimes we seem to have more in common with each other's mothers than we do with our own.

'But we're not Catholic. We're not *anything*.'

'That doesn't matter. They'd love to have you, you're smart, you'll push the results up. Nana can coach you if you're worried; she knows all the saints and the Hail Marys and everything. Hooray, hooray, Bridie's coming to St Marg's!' Stella sang.

We broke into a run across the wet winter grass, whooping and laughing like little kids under the white dawn sky, and Tim bounded after us on his short trundling legs, yapping with delight. It was such a great idea, I even managed to forget about the war.

'Don't forget to ask Lisa!' Stella called as I turned into my street, waving goodbye with the plastic bag that held Tim's poo.

'Let me know if you hear from Jay,' I called back.

When I let myself in, Mum was making coffee in the kitchen. In our house it's just me and Mum. I don't have a dad; never had one; never wanted one, really. It's no big deal. I never even think about it. Mum and I have always been a unit. We have each other, and that's enough. Until lately, anyway. This year, without Stella around, I'd started to notice how busy Mum was with work, how we didn't really do stuff together much anymore. Not that I felt abandoned or resentful or anything. But sometimes I couldn't help wishing Mum would spend a bit more time with me.

I peeled off my parka. The kitchen felt boiling hot after the crisp air outside. It was always hard to drag myself out of bed for our walks, especially in winter, but it was worth the effort for the blood-tingling, alert aliveness afterwards. The radio was muttering in the corner and suddenly I remembered. Soldiers were filing onto planes, weapons were being loaded. Soon, in a faraway country, bombs would fall on streets and houses and families just like ours, blasting their lives apart. The sick feeling flooded back into my stomach.

'Did you hear about the war?' I said.

'I know, it's awful … Pick up your parka, sweetie … Makes me wish I'd marched with you girls on Saturday.'

'Didn't make any difference though, did it?' That was the worst part; all that passion, all that determination – wasted. Useless.

'Maybe it did make a difference. Maybe it made them think twice.'

'What's the use of thinking twice if you go ahead and do it anyway?'

'Fair point. Want some toast?'

'I'm not hungry.'

'Darling, starving yourself won't help anything.'

'Oh, all right.' I sighed. 'Mum? Can I swap over to St Marg's?'

At the toaster, Mum's back froze. Without turning round, she said, 'Why on earth would you want to go there? I thought Stella hated it.'

'She does, but I think … maybe it's because I'm not there. And, you know, I miss her, too.'

'I know you do, darling. It's a shame Mish and Paul got it into their heads …' Mum stopped herself. She turned round and leaned on the bench. 'Maybe you should see this as an opportunity to make some new friends? Not to replace Stella; you and Stella will always be friends, I'm sure.' She could see me opening my mouth to protest. 'But you could broaden your horizons, meet some new people.'

'There aren't any new people, it's the same old people, I know them all already,' I grumbled. 'Couldn't I just try St Marg's and see? We won't know till we do the experiment.' That was Mum's usual line when she was coaxing me to try something new, but it didn't work this time.

'It's halfway through the year, Bridie, it's too disruptive.'

'Change is good,' I said. 'It'll keep me on my toes, challenge me to adapt.' I shadow-boxed round the bench. 'Adapt or perish, isn't that what you say in biology?'

'I'm not sending you to St Margaret's,' snapped Mum. 'You can put that idea right out of your head.'

I stopped boxing. 'Why?'

'Because I'm not. Or any other religious school, for that matter.'

'So if …' I searched my mind for the most prestigious girls' school I could think of, 'if *Brookings Hall* offered me a scholarship, you'd say no?'

'Yes, I would.'

'What's wrong with religious schools?'

'I don't believe in them, on principle. I believe in state-funded, secular education. If people want to teach their children lies and superstition, let them do it at home.' Mum's voice rose, and two red spots glowed in her cheeks.

'But—'

'Bridie, I'm not discussing it. I wouldn't send you to St Margaret's if it was the last school on earth. End of story.'

'But can't we at least *talk* about it?'

'Bridie, I said *enough*.' Mum hadn't spoken to me in that tone of voice since I was about six.

'Right,' I said. 'Fine.' I stalked to the bathroom, fuming. I showered and flung on my school clothes, still silently raging.

How dare she just shut me down like that? *End of story*. She couldn't order me around any more, I was sixteen now. Didn't I get any say in my education, in my own future? My mother was just as bad as the politicians and the dictators, plunging us into war in spite of all our protests. *End of story*. Was that what the Prime Minister said when he made the decision?

The whole world had let me down. Even Mum wouldn't listen to me; how could I expect to stop a war by putting my hand up? Even my best friend was more interested in a boy she'd only just met than in the screwed-up state of the planet. But at least I knew Stella would *listen* to me.

I yelled 'Bye' to Mum as I grabbed my toast and slammed out of the house but I pointedly didn't kiss her before I left. I couldn't wait to talk over the unfairness of it all with Stella. I walked faster and faster to the bus stop where she'd be waiting.

It wasn't till I reached the end of the street that I remembered that Stella was at St Marg's now, that I'd have to get through the whole stupid day without her.

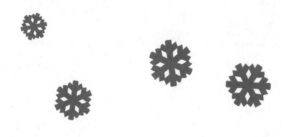

WHEN I GOT home, I felt wrung out. There wasn't anyone at school I could talk to, not properly. No one cared about the war as much as I did. As for the fight with Mum, I couldn't discuss that at all; it would have been kind of insulting to say I wanted to go to another school. Not that I *wanted* to leave, I just wanted to be with Stella. But I knew there was no point bringing it up with Mum again. When she used that voice, the subject was not negotiable. It was so unfair.

Mum didn't get home till late on Mondays. I was supposed to cook dinner but I usually made something pretty lame, like toasted sandwiches. Today there was a sheaf of mail clogging up the letterbox, mostly for Mum, but there was one envelope addressed to me. I was juggling the mail and my schoolbag and wondering who my letter was from, when the phone rang.

'It's me.' Stella was breathless and slightly muffled, trying not to be overheard by Scarlet and Tark. 'He's sent me a *card*.'

I looked down at the square envelope with the unfamiliar handwriting. That was that mystery solved, anyway. He was certainly quick off the mark. I let the envelope drop to the carpet, and flung myself onto the couch. 'What's it say?'

'It says, *Dear Stella, I wanted to thank you for your help on Saturday. I really appreciated your assistance —* he's spelled it with five 'S's, how cute *— I hope we can keep in touch. Best wishes, Jay Ridley.* He wants to keep in touch!'

'That's good,' I said.

'His address is on the envelope, I need you to search the net so we can find his home number.'

Stella has to fight Scarlet and Tark for the internet at home and their computer is in the big back room where anyone can walk past. So any private research like this is my job. 'Okay, hang on.' I could see Jay's address on the back of my own envelope: an outer suburb. At least it was on our side of town. I rolled off the couch. 'I'm switching the computer on now.'

'Did you ask Lisa about swapping schools?'

'She said no way.'

'Oh, nooo! Will you try her again?'

'No, she means it.'

'Bummer,' said Stella, regretful but not devastated. Her head was so full of Jay and his card and his phone number, there wasn't room for anything else; I couldn't burst her bubble by telling her he'd sent me a card too.

'I've got the White Pages up now.' I started to type in the Ridleys' address before Stella read it out.

'Where *is* that?'

'North. Way north. End of the train line north.'

'At least it's our train line,' said Stella cheerfully.

'Well, *nearly* our train line.' I read out the phone number.

'Yay, thanks so much, Bridie. I'm so excited!'

'What are you going to say when you call him?' I had to admire her guts; she wasn't even thinking twice about it.

'I'll wait a couple of days; I don't want to look desperate. Then – this is a genius idea, Bridie – I'll invite him to Bailey Hahn's party.'

'Do you think he'll want to go to a party when he's just been beaten up?'

'He'll have had a week to recover, he'll be all right.' Stella can be ruthless.

'I thought we'd decided not to go to Bailey's party?'

'Nooo! We have to undecide. It's perfect; there'll be heaps of uni people there because of Bailey's brothers. It'll be *sophisticated*. Not just a kids' party with everyone getting trashed and throwing up.'

'Uni people get trashed, too, you know,' I said, but there was no resisting Stella in a mood like this; it was much easier to give in. 'Okay,' I grumbled, and it was lucky Stella couldn't see my limp sprawl across the couch and my total lack of interest in the Stella-and-Jay project, or she would have sacked me as best friend in a blink.

After Stella hung up, I finally opened my own card from Jay.

*Dear Bridie, I wanted to thank you for helping me on Saturday. It was great to meet you. I hope you don't think this is out of line but if you would like to call me some time and hook up, it would be great to thank you properly. It's up to you. Thank you again for your help, Jay.*

Did he mean *hook up* like the rest of the world meant *hook up*? 'Cause, if so, that was taking things pretty fast, too fast for me. And there was his phone number, the same number I'd just looked up on the net. The number he hadn't sent to Stella.

*Oh dear*, I thought. This could get messy.

But I was too tired to think about it, and I had homework, and I had to get dinner, so I threw the card into a drawer. Anyway, it wasn't possible that Jay could like me better than Stella – Stella's the pretty one. I'm short and frizzy-haired and just generally blah. Maybe he was concussed and he'd mixed our names up. That would be it.

*And anyway*, I thought. *I bet he doesn't come.*


Well, I was wrong about that, too.

'He's *definitely* coming.' Stella stretched her lips in front of the mirror and carefully painted them with gloss. 'Is this colour all right? Do I look okay?'

'You look amazing,' I said honestly. We were getting ready at her place, with Scarlet and Tark goggling from the ends of the beds. The deal was that Mish would take us there and Mum would pick us up and Stella would stay over at our place. We'd even swapped dog-walk days with Tark.

It was always pretty chaotic at the Kincaids'. Their house was the same size as ours, more or less, but they had to squeeze in five people and a dog, though he was a small dog. Stella and Scarlet shared a bedroom, and Tark's room was a glorified cupboard. There was always heaps of noise and kids rushing in and out. The TV was always on, though Mish would switch it off whenever she walked past. There was Scarlet tooting her flute, and Paul booming away and striding off to his next meeting, shedding papers as he went. Paul was on about a zillion committees: school council, cricket club, a charity for the homeless, something else about refugees. I guess that was how Stella got political. Which was how *I* got political.

Stella painted around her eyes. 'Jay said his brother's dropping him off on the way to uni and picking him up on the way back, so he'll be there pretty early.'

My heart skipped, just for a second, at the possibility of seeing Jay's good-looking brother. Which was dumb, because we *wouldn't*. And he *wouldn't* stop in for a drink. He was probably on P-plates – he couldn't be older than twenty-one.

I was wearing my normal party clothes, dark jeans and a T-shirt. I'd done my eyes, and tried to slick my hair down, though that never really works, it always bounces up again. But Stella had gone all out – tights, micro-mini, plunging shirt, heaps of make-up, and everything kind of silvery-shimmery. With her pale eyes and hair, she looked like a water-sprite or a ghost. Standing side by side, we looked bizarre: one long and silver, one short and dark, as if I were Stella's stumpy shadow.

'I look *weird*,' I wailed, though what I meant was that next to Stella, I looked clunky, ordinary.

Stella surveyed me thoughtfully. 'That T-shirt's not tight enough. Here, try this. And you need lips. Scar, get Mum's red lipstick, you know, the RED red.'

Scarlet scrambled to obey; she was more excited about this party than I was. Two minutes later, I was a vampire with very obvious boobs. Amazing what a too-small T-shirt and a slash of RED red lipstick can do. Stella must have picked up some tips about clothes and lipstick from the giggling morons, so St Marg's hadn't been a complete waste of time.

Tark gazed at Stella in awe. 'You look *pretty*.'

'I don't want to look pretty, I want to look sexy. I wish I had your boobs, Bridie.' Stella frowned at her reflection, then sighed. 'Oh, well. Let's go.'

We were way too early, of course. Even Mish looked dubious when we said we were ready to go, but Stella didn't want to miss Jay, or risk him meeting someone else before we arrived. I was still privately convinced he wouldn't show up at all.

Mish dropped us off at Bailey's respectable suburban house. Music was thumping dully from within, and two security guards and a couple of dads were stationed outside to deal with gatecrashers.

'Stella! Jay hasn't got an invitation!'

Stella rolled her eyes at me. 'I got one from Bailey and express-posted it.' When Stella was this determined to make something work, there was no stopping her. I almost felt sorry for poor old unsuspecting Jay. First beaten up by thugs, then steam-rollered by Stella. I didn't know which would be worse.

We presented our invites and walked inside. A knot of guests shot hostile stares at us from a corner of the almost-empty living room as we came in, and returned to their murmured conversation. We didn't know any of them. For a sinking moment I wanted to ring Mum and tell her to come and pick us up. But Stella was made of steelier stuff.

'Come on, the action's in the kitchen.' She pushed me ahead; I felt like a tank, all lips and chest.

Stella was right. There was a noisy crush in the kitchen. Outside, guests were clustered under overhead braziers on the deck, scattered around the pool and the snack table.

'I can't see anyone I know!' I yelled to Stella.

Stella was looking around, but of course she was only interested in finding one person and it didn't look as if he was here yet. Clearly it was really Bailey's brother's party; everyone here was older than us. I felt like a kid in dress-ups, with my stupid red lips and my stupid thrusting chest. 'I look ridiculous; I'm going to wash my mouth off.'

Stella grabbed me. 'You stay right there. Your mouth is fine, you look gorgeous.'

Which was kind, because next to Stella in her silver top, I was nothing.

We hadn't brought anything to drink. We couldn't have fooled Mish, even if we'd wanted to. But there was a big bowl of punch on the bench with bits of fruit floating in it, and Stella ladled us each a plastic cup. I took a big nervous swallow and nearly choked; it burned the back of my throat.

Tears sprang to Stella's eyes. 'Vodka?' she coughed.

'Just a dash,' I whispered hoarsely.

'Are we going to get *drunk* tonight, Bridie Vandenberg?'

I shut my eyes, feeling as if that question had already been settled as far as I was concerned. The floor was tilting under my feet. I shook my head vigorously.

Stella took another gulp and eyed me sideways. 'Then let's just get *tipsy*.'

31

'Absolutely,' I said.

Stella refilled her cup, which she'd emptied with startling speed. 'That's very funny. Absolutely. Absolut vodka, get it?'

'Oh. Yeah.' I took a second cautious sip. It still burned.

Stella topped up her cup again, which didn't strike me as such a great idea, and we stepped out onto the deck.

After the steamy hubbub of the kitchen, the chill of the night air and the gassy heat that shimmered from the braziers made me giddy. I found myself next to a bowl of corn chips. As my eyes scanned the crowd, my hand went back and forth to my mouth and before I knew it the bowl was half-empty. Not a great look. But in retrospect I'm glad I had the chip bowl because all Stella had was the punch.

'Hi,' said a shy voice behind us and we both spun round to see Jay grinning down at us. His eye was still bandaged, though less thickly than at the hospital.

'Oh my God, your poor eye!' cried Stella.

Jay fidgeted uncomfortably. 'It's okay. They're going to do some more tests. And I have to wear this for a while.' He touched the bandage sheepishly. 'But, you know, I always wanted to be a pirate.'

'How are you?' I said. 'How are your ribs?'

'Cracked, not broken. Hurts when I laugh. So don't be funny, okay?' He had a very sweet smile.

'You look really *well*!' Stella gushed. 'Considering you had the bejesus kicked out of you.'

Jay looked even more uncomfortable, and I wondered why. 'It would have been worse if you guys hadn't come along,' he said.

Now it was our turn to fidget awkwardly.

'Want a drink?' said Stella, slopping her punch.

Jay shook his head. 'I don't— I can't—'

'He's probably on fifty different kinds of medication,' I said.

'Oh, yeah. Soft drink, then?'

'Thanks,' said Jay, and Stella scooted off, stumbling against the snack table as she went.

That left me and Jay alone together.

'It's good to see you,' he said shyly.

He meant both of us, no doubt. 'It's good you could come,' I said, and then I got stuck.

'I can't stay too long,' said Jay. 'Elliot's picking me up.'

'Yeah, Stella said.' My hand groped among the corn chips and I stuffed a fistful into my mouth, scattering crumbs everywhere. What was it that Stella had said about being sophisticated?

Then, thank God, Stella returned with a lemonade for Jay and a fresh cup of punch for herself, and she took over. Jay and I only had to stand there while she chattered and played with her hair and spilled her punch down her top; she did all the work.

She complimented Jay on his detective work in tracking her down; she asked him what he planned to do after Year 12. He said he wanted to travel for a while, maybe to America, and think about it, which was a fairly cool answer. She told him what she and I were doing and our plans – architecture for Stella, arts for me; she asked about Elliot and did he like Law. I tried to look nonchalant, which should have been easy, because I didn't even *know* Elliot. She asked how long they'd lived where they lived – they'd moved there for their dad's work five years ago.

I had to hand it to Stella; I couldn't have thought up half those questions. Someone came by with a fistful of raspberry Breezers and Stella grabbed one; I was still nursing my first cup of punch. I was half listening to see if Jay called Stella Bridie, to confirm my theory that he'd mixed our names up, but he didn't. He just stood beside me, sipping his lemonade and smiling his soft, shy smile.

The party grew louder and louder around us, and Stella's questions became shriller and less coherent. After a while I noticed that she wasn't listening to Jay's replies. Her eyes flickered around and she swigged from her drink. She'd laugh for no reason and shoot out another question, even if Jay hadn't finished answering the last one. And at last, slightly befuddled by the punch myself, I realised Stella was completely, totally, utterly, horribly wasted.

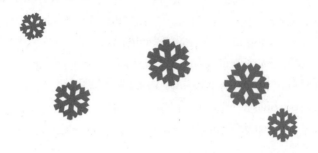

JUST AT THAT moment, Stella lurched forward and clutched Jay's sleeve. 'Dance with me, Jay,' she purred, running her hand up and down his arm, and tilting her head sideways.

I tried to step back but I was trapped by the table. Then I noticed that Jay's one green-gold eye was wide in panic.

'I can't dance,' he murmured, gesturing vaguely to his ribs, but Stella's fingers tightened round his arm and she began to drag him to the end of the deck where people were swaying to the music.

'Come *on*, Jay.' Her voice was too loud and her eyes were unfocussed, and a couple of buttons on her top had popped open, giving the whole world a great view of her bra. 'C'mon, Jay, I saved your life, can't you have a little dance with me?'

Jay shot me a terrified look over his shoulder and I reached for Stella's other hand.

'Jay doesn't want to dance yet,' I said. 'Let's get some water; that punch has gone straight to my head.'

But Stella shook me off. 'I want to dance!' she cried, much too shrilly. Faces turned in our direction and a couple of the older guys sniggered. One of them called, 'You go, girl!' as Stella staggered onto the dance floor. She waved her arms in the air and swung her long hair in wild circles.

'Woo!' she shouted. 'C'mon, Jay, dance with me!'

'She's not normally like this,' I said helplessly to Jay. 'She's just ... nervous.'

'Is that what it's called?' said Jay, with a small, worried smile.

Stella spun an unsteady pirouette and knocked an entwined couple off the deck.

'Hey, watch it!' yelled the guy.

*Oh, great*, I thought. *Now it's Stella's turn to get beaten up.*

But Stella didn't last long on the dance floor. Inevitably, with the spinning and the head-shaking and the alcohol, her stomach rebelled. She staggered off the deck and swayed toward the pool. For one horrible second I thought she was going to fall in. But she sank abruptly to her knees at the pool's edge, delicately held her hair back with both hands, and threw up into the water.

That was when Bailey Hahn decided to appear – the first time I'd seen him all night. He planted himself in front of me, hands on hips. 'She's got to go.'

'Go?' I echoed blankly.

He jerked his thumb. 'Out, now. Come on, Bridie, it's embarrassing. She's totally trashed and it's only half-past nine.'

'She's not the only one!' I waved my hand at random people around the garden.

Bailey thrust his face close to mine. I wouldn't have lit

a match to his breath, either. 'She's thrown up in the *pool*! That's disgusting.'

I craned round him to see Stella, who'd rolled onto her back and was laughing weakly, hysterically, up at the sky. 'Okay, we'll go, just let me —' I shoved past Bailey and ran to help Stella up. She lolled against me, her breath stinking of vomit.

'You're my friend,' she murmured. 'Oh, Bridie, I love you …'

'Yeah, me too, whatever …'

Then I realised that Jay was there, holding her up on the other side.

'I've got to get her home.' I blinked back tears. In Bailey's crowd, it was okay to be drunk, it was even sort of cool, but throwing up was a definite no-no, especially for a girl, and especially this early in the night. I bet Bailey himself would be chucking his guts up before the party was over, and in the morning he'd be bragging like a hero. But Stella overdoing the punch – that was a crime.

Everyone drew back as if we were toxic. Everyone except Jay; he was right there with his arm round Stella, vomit and all. 'I have to call my mum,' I said. 'Oh, no—'

'What's wrong?'

'Mum's not home till ten. We never thought we'd leave so early. I can't ring Stella's parents; they can't see her like this.' The music pounded in my ears, the deck was throbbing. I didn't know what to do.

'I could call my brother,' suggested Jay in his soft, calm voice, and I swear I could have kissed him.

'Oh, Jay, I love you,' murmured Stella, leaning against his chest, and Jay flushed sunburn-pink beneath his bandages.

Bailey Hahn muscled in again. 'I mean it, Bridie, you've got to leave now.'

'Or what? You'll call security?' Then it occurred to me that he could do exactly that.

'Just let me clean her up, okay?' I snapped, and together Jay and I led Stella inside. I pushed her into a bathroom and sponged her face and made her rinse her mouth. She threw up again, in the toilet this time, thankfully, but when we emerged, she was looking pretty white.

Jay was waiting. He offered Stella his arm and escorted her through the crowd as if they were the prince and princess leaving the ball.

'Thanks for a wonderful party,' he said politely to Bailey's dad, who was hovering at the door, presumably gearing himself up to kick us out, or maybe just checking that Stella didn't heave on the good cushions on the way.

'Yeah, it was fabulous.' I swept past. 'Great idea, tipping all that vodka in the punch.'

Stella waved blearily at everyone from Jay's arm. She stumbled at the door and I thought she was going to crash down the steps, but Jay and I steadied her. We made it onto the footpath and some way down the street without major injury. Then Stella kind of swooned onto the nature strip, giggling, and Jay sat down abruptly, clutching his side.

'Oh, no, your ribs! I'm so sorry. I forgot …'

'Not your fault.' He winced. 'Hurts though. Elliot's on his way. Probably about fifteen minutes.'

'Thanks so much, Jay. I don't know what to say. Stella's not … She's never done this before, truly.'

Jay didn't say anything. He sat on the grass beneath a streetlight, looking at me. I felt my face glow hot. Stella was lying flat on her back a short distance away, crooning softly to herself.

'You're a good friend,' he said at last.

'I never wanted to go to this stupid party in the first place!' I blurted. 'I'm not … I'm not really a party person.'

'Me neither,' said Jay. 'Not this kind of party.' He turned away and mumbled, 'I've never been to a party like that before.'

'I don't think I ever will again, after tonight,' I said. 'And I'm pretty sure Stella – well, maybe Stella will. I guess she won't remember much about it.'

Jay smiled his quiet smile and I found myself liking him more and more. 'Elliot talked my parents into letting me come. He said I should see for myself what it was like.' He nodded towards Stella, who'd fallen silent, gazing dreamily up at the clouds. 'I don't understand why anyone would do that to themselves.'

'Fun?' I said vaguely, and we caught each other's eye and laughed. Jay clutched his ribs. 'Oh, sorry!'

'Sneezing's the worst,' he said. Then, very seriously, 'Bridie.'

So he did know my name. 'Hello.'

'There's something you ought to know about me. Something pretty important.'

*Oh, God*, I thought. *He's gay? He's got a terminal illness? He's going overseas? He's married?* – I don't know where that last one came from. 'Okay,' I said in a nervous squeak.

'I just think, you know, if we're going to get to know each other better … I mean, I don't know if you, if you want to be friends, but …'

'Okay, what?'

He took a deep breath. 'I'm a Christian.'

There was a pause.

'Oh,' I said weakly at last. 'Okay. A Christian … wow.'

It explained so much. The way he flinched when Stella blasphemed, the not drinking, the awkward way he'd looked around at the party, as if he'd landed among aliens. Hook up? Of course he didn't mean *hook up*. He was a total innocent.

But … in a nice way.

Behind us, music throbbed dully from the Hahns' house. A car roared past, stopped for an instant, disgorged a knot of party guests with a flurry of slammed doors, and roared away. Stella was singing again, a Zita Mariposa song: *the taste of honey is on your lips; your tongue is honey for me.*

Jay said, 'Bridie? You're not saying anything.'

'I'm just getting used to it. I thought you were going to say you were a werewolf or something. A Christian, that's … interesting.'

'I was scared to tell you. I thought you and Stella would think it was uncool. I was … I guess I was embarrassed. And tonight, when I saw your friends …'

'They're not *my* friends,' I said quickly. 'Not really Stella's either, she only knows Bailey from soccer.'

There was a pause.

'You really think it's interesting?'

'Yeah.' I thought about it. 'Yeah, I do. I don't know much about God and religion and … everything.' As far as I knew, I'd never met a Christian before, not a proper one. Apart from Nana Kincaid. And Jay and Nana Kincaid were *not* the same thing.

Jay cleared his throat. 'If you wanted to, you could come to our church, check it out? My dad's the pastor – Pastor Matt. It's Northside Church, have you heard of it? And Elliot's a youth leader.'

'So it's a family affair.'

'Yeah, kind of … anyway, you're welcome to come along.'

My mouth was open to say, *thanks but no thanks, I'm not really a church person*, but instead I heard myself say, 'Okay, maybe I will.' The vodka must have still been racing round my veins; but the weird thing was, at that moment, I *was* interested. Since the war was declared, there'd been a lot of talk about God – our God and their God – so maybe it was time to find out what all the fuss was about.

'Stella's welcome, too. Do you think she'd come?'

'She *might*.' I looked doubtfully over my shoulder to where she was lying on the grass, singing to herself. 'I'll ask her.' I glanced sideways at Jay. 'It's interesting to meet someone who … believes in something.'

'It would be so great if you could both come,' said Jay earnestly. 'I'm sure God sent you for a reason. You know, last Saturday. You saved me. Wouldn't it be amazing if I helped save you?'

'Um … yeah.' I didn't know what to make of that. Saved? From what exactly, what did that mean?

An old blue car drew up to the kerb and Jay jumped to his feet. 'Elliot! Over here!'

'Hi there,' said a dry voice, and Elliot leaned out the window. I scrambled up and brushed myself off. 'Got a casualty, have we?'

'She had a bit too much to drink,' I said.

Elliot grimaced. 'Think she'll chuck in my car?'

'I don't *think* so,' I said cautiously. 'She's been sick twice, I'm pretty sure it's all gone.'

'Nice,' said Elliot. 'All right, hop in. I suppose you want to sober her up before you take her home? We'd better find a cafe.'

I hauled Stella to her feet and she weaved her way over to the car. '*Hi!*' she said brightly to Elliot. 'Have we met before?'

'You might want to—' Elliot gestured to his chest.

I thought he meant me; involuntarily I glanced down, my cheeks burning.

'Her top,' said Elliot. 'Before we go anywhere in public?'

'Oh, right.' Hastily I buttoned Stella back into her shirt and shoved her into the car. 'This is really nice of you,' I burbled as I struggled to fasten Stella's seatbelt.

Elliot shrugged as he pulled out into the street. 'What goes around,' he said enigmatically, and ruffled his brother's hair. 'How are you, mate?' he asked quietly.

'Yeah, good,' said Jay, but he sat there in silence, either from exhaustion or shyness or sheer embarrassment, while Stella sang along to the radio and told us all how much she loved us, and Elliot drove on grimly, a scowl set on his face.

He found a cafe and we poured herbal tea and water into Stella and she started to look less pale and more connected to reality.

'Make her drink plenty of water before she goes to bed,' said Elliot. 'You staying at her place?'

'She's staying at mine.'

'Good. She'll be pretty sick in the morning.' He said to Jay, 'Drink up, mate. We've got an early start.'

Jay swilled his hot chocolate. 'First service is at ten,' he told me. 'Dad likes us to go.'

Elliot's eyebrow shot up; obviously he was surprised Jay had told us about their church. Perhaps he knew from experience that it wasn't the world's best pick-up line.

'You can come, too, if you like,' said Jay.

'I don't think they'll be going anywhere tomorrow morning, Jay,' said Elliot, and he flicked a quick sceptical glance at me that said more clearly than words that he didn't expect us to turn up to their church *ever*. I stared right back; he might get a big shock one day.

The whole exchange went right over Stella's head; she was squinting at a sugar tube. 'How do they get the sugar *in* there? It's such a weeny little hole ...'

Elliot threw some money on the table. 'Let's go,' he growled. 'The Elliot Ridley Taxi Service turns into a pumpkin at midnight.'

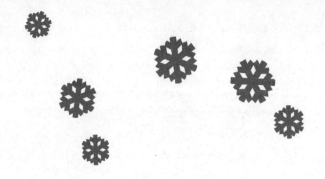

MUM WAS SURPRISED to see us. 'I told you to call, I was waiting,' she said. 'I don't like you taking lifts from strange men.'

Mum worries too much. I nearly told her Elliot was a church youth leader but I wasn't ready to break that news to Stella yet. Instead I said, 'He wasn't a stranger, he was Jay's brother, the guy from the peace rally.'

'That *is* a stranger. Next time—' Mum broke off as Stella gave a huge yawn and sagged against the wall. Her eye make-up was all smudged; she looked like a skinny, bedraggled panda. Suddenly I was so tired I could hardly stand up either.

Mum raised her hands. 'Off you go. And plenty of water before you—'

'Before we go to bed, yeah, yeah, I've got the message.' I pushed Stella into my room and she promptly collapsed onto the bed and began to snore. I had to wake her up to tip a bottle of water down her throat before she passed out again. I toppled onto the spare mattress like a fallen tree, and suddenly it was morning.

Stella's pale, panda face gave me an agonised stare over the edge of the bed. She whispered, 'Tell me it was all a bad dream?'

I rolled over in my sleeping-bag and pretended to think hard. 'Hmm, let's see … No, pretty much all true, I'm afraid.'

'Oh, *God.*' Stella's face abruptly vanished. Her disembodied voice begged, 'Which parts?'

'The getting trashed part, the flirting with Jay part, the throwing up in the pool part—'

'Okay, stop! Ow, my head. I feel terrible.' There was a pause. 'I threw up in the *pool?*'

'Mmm. But on the plus side, guess what? Jay's a born-again Christian.'

'You *what?* You're joking. Bridie, this a joke, right?'

'Well, he's some kind of Christian. He told me while we were waiting for Elliot to pick us up.'

'Oh, yeah, Elliot … I remember now … Jay's a *Christian?*' Another pause. 'So I guess he was really impressed with the whole getting-wasted, throwing-up thing?'

'He was cool, actually.' I propped myself on my elbow, thinking back. 'He called Elliot to get us, and he was really sweet to you.'

'Yeah?' said Stella hopefully. 'What did he do?'

'Um …' Maybe that was a stretch. 'He invited us to his church?'

'How romantic,' groaned Stella. 'I can't believe I've got a crush on a *Christian.*'

I noted that her feelings for Jay had already been downgraded from 'in love' to mere 'crush'. For some perverse reason this annoyed me.

'He's still the same person,' I said crossly; my head was throbbing too. 'Just because he goes to church, so what? Just because he believes in something.'

'Hey.' Stella pointed her finger at me. 'I'm the one who goes to Catholic school, remember? I've got enough Christians in my life without adding to the collection.'

'I told him we'd think about it.'

'About *going to church*? Are you crazy?'

'He's nice. Elliot's nice. How bad can it be?'

Stella squinted at me. 'You've never been to church, have you? I have, heaps of times, with Nana, and it's *God-awful*.'

It took a second for that to sink in, then we both giggled.

'I suppose that's exactly what it's meant to be,' I said. 'Godly and full of awe.'

'Shut up and get out of my way.' Stella swung her legs over the bed. 'I feel *sick*.'

We went back and forth on it a few times over the next week. Stella was torn between being so mortified that she never wanted to see Jay again, and wanting to show him what a nice wholesome girl she really was. I guess I was just intrigued. I did genuinely like Jay (and Elliot, sort of – not that that was relevant). I thought it was gutsy of Jay to confess something so deeply uncool, and I was curious. No one had ever offered to introduce me to God before.

We looked up Northside Church on the internet on Monday

night, before Mum came home. After her rant about religious schools, I wasn't about to tell her I was considering going to an actual church.

'Wow, it's big. They've got branches all over the city.'

'It's a franchise, it's the Chicken Hut of churches … look!' Stella's finger stabbed Elliot's photo on the screen. 'There's grumpy-pants.'

'Youth Outreach Program,' I read. 'Do you think they're just trying to recruit us?'

'Der! That's what Christians *do*. That's their job – they convert people.'

In the end, we decided to go. I stayed over at Stella's on Saturday, which wasn't unusual, but I didn't exactly tell Mum what our plans were for Sunday. We worked out that we could catch the train and walk to the church; it was right at the end of the line.

'Dress up,' ordered Stella. 'Nice frocks. Nana always made me wear a nice frock when we went to Mass.'

Seeing as how we weren't six years old any more, we couldn't quite stretch to nice frocks, but we both wore skirts and tights. Knee-length skirts. I wore a neat buttoned-up shirt and Stella wore a skivvy. 'Very modest,' she said with satisfaction, turning in front of the mirror. I felt as if we were dressing up as nuns – not the old-fashioned sort, with headdresses and flowing robes, but boring modern nuns, in cardigans, with bad hair.

'Have you noticed how Christians always have bad hair?' said Stella when we were on the train at last.

'God doesn't care what they look like,' I said. 'He wants

them to worry about helping other people, not trivial things like hair.'

'Look who's the expert now!'

'Shut up,' I mumbled. Okay, maybe I had read the Northside website, maybe I'd done a little Christian research. I didn't understand a lot of it, but the parts about helping others and being grateful for the world made sense to me. Wasn't that what Stella and I believed in? Only we called it being 'politically active' and 'environmentally aware'.

'Anyway,' I added. 'Jay's got good hair.'

'Huh,' said Stella.

We nearly got lost between the station and the church. Stella has a problem with left and right; according to her, I have a problem with east and west. We were still bickering when we found it: a big, low, grey-brown building with an enormous cross on the front wall, and a sea of cars all around, and a swarm of people hurrying inside.

'Wow,' said Stella. 'It's bigger than St John's, where Nana goes.'

We hung back, watching, both suddenly shy and self-conscious. Our clothes were totally wrong. We'd got the modest skirts right, but I'd never seen so much cleavage. Everyone was certainly dressed up, but not in 'nice frocks'. I felt like an idiot in my chaste shirt and lace-up shoes. I was on the verge of whispering *let's go* to Stella, when Jay shouted our names.

He was wearing a proper black eye-patch, waving and grinning from ear to ear. 'I can't believe you came! Wow, you look … different.' He glanced at his watch. 'We're about to

48

start. We all sit down the front. My family, I mean. Do you want to sit with us?'

'Um … I think we'd feel more comfortable up the back, for our first time,' said Stella.

'Sure.' Jay smiled again and patted us each on the shoulder. 'It's *great* to see you guys. Meet you after, yeah?' And he rushed off. He seemed so confident and relaxed in his natural habitat, not shy at all. It was Stella and me who'd turned awkward.

'I think you're forgiven,' I said to Stella. 'I think your sins have been washed away.'

Stella pulled a face. 'Funny. S'pose we'd better go in.'

I don't know what I was expecting – not so many people, that's for sure. The building was more like a big theatre than my idea of a church, with the audience in tiered seats facing a stage with another huge cross hung above it. Stella and I found seats at the back, and as soon as we sat down, music began to blast from speakers all around the walls.

It was *weird*. Like a rock concert, only all the songs were about God and Jesus. There was a choir on stage, and a full-on band, plus a guy with a microphone and a pretty good voice, who led the singing. It was all mercy and glory and being saved and rejoicing.

The whole crowd was on their feet, singing their lungs out, clapping and swaying. The words were projected up on a big screen, and a couple of times I found my feet tapping and my lips moving. The music was so infectious that it was hard not to let it carry me away. But Stella stood with her arms folded, stonily silent.

49

In a strange way, the atmosphere reminded me of the peace rally: that united feeling, that sense of being part of something bigger than my own small self. Except this time, Stella and I were outsiders, not part of the Northside worship-beast.

But I had the feeling that it would be easy to slip inside, easy to belong. Every time I looked around, someone smiled right at me – an Asian woman, a red-haired girl about our age, a burly Islander man, a bald guy. This crowd was just as diverse as the peace marchers, and everyone was smiling and singing and being friendly and happy. And gradually I started to relax into it, I let myself be absorbed. By the end I was singing along with everyone else. But when Stella glared at me I stopped, even though we were more conspicuous standing there in silence than joining in.

At last, Pastor Matt, Jay and Elliot's dad, stood up to speak. He had a wonderful voice, deep and ringing and utterly sincere. He was quite handsome for an old guy; you could see where Jay and Elliot got it from. And he made jokes, too.

I don't know what I'd been expecting him to talk about – sin and damnation and hellfire, maybe, not that I had a clear idea what any of those things were. But instead he talked about love. He talked about saving the world through love. He talked about how God is our loving father, and how He sent His son Jesus to be our friend, the best friend we could ever have, a friend who would never desert us. A friend who brought a message of love to save the world, a message that could come alive in us, every moment of every day. And finally He reminded us that we could help contribute to the work of Jesus, by cash or cheque or credit card, and we'd find envelopes under our seats.

There was thunderous applause, then more singing and clapping. Other people were groping under their seats, and in a daze, I did the same. I slipped a five-dollar note into the envelope and held it out to Stella, but she frowned and shook her head. A man came along and collected the envelopes, and whispered, 'May the blessing of the Lord be on your head,' and he smiled so warmly I felt a bit of a fraud. I mean, it was only five dollars. But I guess even five dollars multiplied by every person in that church was a fair amount of money – and I saw one old lady put in a hundred.

Afterwards we hung around outside in the winter sunshine, waiting for Jay. I kept half an eye out for Elliot too, just casually, but I didn't see him. Stella had her arms folded. At last Jay wriggled through the crowd and rushed up to us, beaming. 'So, what did you think?'

He was asking me. I saw Stella's face close up.

'Your dad's a great speaker,' I said.

'Amazing,' said Stella, just on the line between sarcastic and sincere.

'You should really come to youth group,' said Jay, still looking at me. 'It's cool, you'd love it. Wednesday nights, seven till nine.'

Stella said, 'I can't. Not Wednesdays.'

'I don't know …' I said awkwardly,

'This week we're having a debate about the war,' said Jay,

as if he knew that would hook me in. He barely even glanced at Stella. It was the first time a boy had ever shown more interest in me than her. It felt all wrong, but at the same time, not unpleasant.

Jay laid his hand on my arm and said in a low voice, 'I'd really like you to come.'

I swallowed. 'I'll … I'll think about it.'

Stella said firmly, 'We have to go now. My nana's coming for lunch, we'll be late. Come on, Bridie.'

'Call me!' Jay yelled after us.


As we waited on the station platform, Stella said abruptly, 'You won't go back, will you?'

'I don't know. It wasn't what I expected. They all seemed really nice. It was … interesting.'

'You think?' Stella snorted. 'Well, *I'm* not coming, that's for sure. Sheesh. I just don't get it.'

'Get what?'

'I just can't *believe* in all that. To me, it's the same as saying, let's all believe in Greek myths, let's believe in Gods and Goddesses living in the clouds and throwing down thunderbolts. We don't believe in that stuff anymore, so how can you believe there's an old man called God up there somewhere, looking down at us? And he had a son called Jesus who died, then came back to life? Where's the *evidence*, people? It's the tooth fairy, it's the Easter bunny.'

'Okay,' I said slowly. 'When you put it like that, it does sound … unlikely. But what about what Pastor Matt said today, the message of Jesus? Love one another. That's pretty radical. If everyone lived by that, it would change the world. No more wars, no more poverty. Maybe you don't need to get into the whole rose-from-the-dead, died-for-our-sins bit.'

Stella leaned out to see if the train was coming. 'That's another thing I don't get. Jesus died for our sins, what does that *mean*?'

'He died so we could have eternal life, isn't that what Pastor Matt said?'

'But if God loves us so much, why not just *give* us eternal life? What's the point of killing Jesus?' Stella shook her head. 'I tell you what, if I was Jesus, I'd be way mad with my dad.'

I laughed, though I felt a bit guilty. I was pretty sure the gang at Northside wouldn't think it was funny.

'Oh, well,' said Stella, as the train finally roared into the station. 'When you go to *youth group*, you can ask them all about it.'

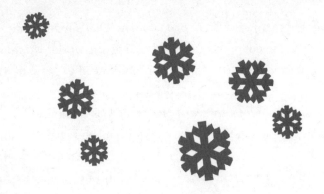

THE KINCAIDS' HOUSE was mayhem as usual. Scarlet was playing the flute to Nana, Tark was watching cartoons, Paul lumbered up and down the hallway booming into the phone, while Mish whirled about the kitchen in the corner of the big room, preparing lunch.

'Stella, could you be an angel and make a salad? Bridie, is there milk in the fridge?'

I had a peek. 'Nup.'

'Damn – *Paul!* When you're finished – bread and milk.'

Paul nodded; he raised his hand, grinned at me and said into the phone, 'I understand that, mate, but the point is …'

'Should I go?' I offered, but Mish shook her head.

'Sit there and talk to me. Use the other tomatoes, Stella, don't waste them.'

'But they're yucky,' said Stella.

'They're all right. Cut the bad bits out.'

'I'm going!' yelled Paul, and the door banged behind him.

'Mish tells me you've been at church,' said Nana Kincaid,

who'd escaped from Scarlet and pulled out a chair at the dining table.

'It was boring.' Stella chopped tomatoes. 'I hate church.'

'Stella!'

'Well, I do.'

Nana shook her head. 'Show some respect. Priests and nuns give up so much to do God's work.'

'They chose it, no one asked them to.'

'*God* asked them to,' said Nana. 'And don't you roll your eyes at me.'

I started to lay the table, listening to them argue. Mish caught my eye and we exchanged a smile.

'Nana, the church is so *sexist*! Why is God called Him? Why shouldn't God be female? Why can't women be priests?'

'Because Jesus was a man.'

'Why does a priest need a penis, he's not even allowed to use it!'

'*Stella!*' But Nana Kincaid couldn't help smiling.

Stella scraped the tomatoes into a salad bowl. 'There aren't enough priests to go round. They're all old and doddery, and the church still won't let women do it. It's cutting out fifty per cent of the human race; it's saying women aren't *capable*. That's a terrible message to send to girls.'

'Mother Teresa was a woman. The Blessed Virgin Mary was a woman.'

'So we're allowed to be saints? We're allowed to be virgins? But that's all?'

'Of course not, you can be a wife and a mother and—'

'Nana! I want more out of my life than *that*.'

Mish made an indistinct sound, half laugh, half snort, and quickly smothered it.

'Women are different,' said Nana comfortably. 'You'll understand when you're older.'

Stella gave up on the salad and faced her grandmother with her hands on her hips, knife still clenched in her fist. 'What about all the terrible things the church has done? The crusades, the Inquisition, burning people at the stake. What about child abuse? What about forbidding men to wear condoms, even to stop spreading AIDS?'

'Christianity has been around for two thousand years, of course it isn't perfect. But look at all the wonderful work the churches have done through the ages, all over the world: taking care of the sick, the homeless, the poor; educating children; feeding the starving. And churches give hope. They help millions of people. They give care and love.'

'That's what Bridie said,' snorted Stella, and Nana Kincaid turned to me with her pale blue eyes as bright and sharp as Stella's own in her soft velvety face.

'Ah, Bridie. You've always had more sense than Stella.'

I muttered something, uncomfortably caught between Stella and Nana, and then Mish rescued me.

'Sit down everyone – oh, Paul, there you are. Thanks, darling – Tark, cut some bread; you're so good at it.'

We all scraped back chairs, sat down and began to help ourselves to food. Tark was talking about football, and Nana had just asked me about school when Stella started up again.

'If church is so fantastic, how come Dad stopped going?'

Scarlet groaned. 'Give it a rest, Stella!'

Paul reached for the bread. 'I still believe the Church does good work in the community, and I still want to help with that.'

'But you don't go to Mass any more.'

'No. I have theological difficulties.'

'What does that mean?' I asked.

Nana Kincaid didn't say anything, but she had a pained expression on her face.

Paul waved his fork. 'The virgin birth, the miracles, heaven and hell, transubstantiation—'

'Trans-*what?*'

'That's when the bread and wine at Communion turn into the body and blood of Christ.'

'Eew!' squealed Stella.

Tark said flatly, 'Yuck.'

'Not *literally*,' I said.

'Well, yes. According to Catholic scholars, the essential substance of the bread and wine literally becomes Christ's flesh and blood. Like magic. You can see why I have trouble believing it – sorry, Mum.' Paul pulled an apologetic face at Nana. 'Not to mention confession and the resurrection and the blessed martyrs and the rosary.'

Nana carved up her asparagus tart. 'You say what you like. You'll come back in the end. They always do.'

'Huh!' said Stella. 'Not this little black duck.'

I said to Paul, 'If you don't believe it, why are you sending Stella to St Margaret's?'

'Good question,' said Stella.

'I'd *like* to believe it,' said Paul, and laughed. 'I do believe in the moral side of it. The Ten Commandments, do unto others, turn the other cheek. I believe in *that*. And St Margaret's has an excellent music program.'

Stella rolled her eyes.

I turned to Mish. 'Do you believe in God?'

Mish laughed. 'Me? I'm a wishy-washy New Age mystic. I believe in nothing and everything. I'm not a huge fan of organised religion. But I do believe in ghosts, and karma, and the power of prayer – even if I'm not sure there's anyone there to hear it.' She pointed her knife emphatically. 'But I must say, I'm very happy to see you girls exploring your spirituality.'

Stella made gagging noises, and Nana snorted, and they looked at each other and laughed. They loved to argue, but deep down, they were exactly the same.


When I got home, Mum was in her study marking papers. I brought her a cup of tea.

'Thanks, darling, that's sweet of you.'

'I do have an ulterior motive.' I leaned against the doorway. 'Could you give me a lift on Wednesday night? About half-past six?'

'I suppose so. Where to?'

I named the suburb where the church was.

'What on earth's all the way out there?'

'It's this youth group thing,' I mumbled.

Mum frowned. 'What kind of youth group?'

I drew on the floor with my shoe. 'It's called Northside.'

'But what is it, some political thing?'

I took a deep breath. 'It's a church group.'

'A *what*?'

'It's that boy, Jay, you know, the one who went to the party? Well, he and his brother are part of this church and Stella and I went along and it was kind of – anyway, they have a youth group and this week they're talking about the war and I just thought it'd be interesting, you know, to get a different perspective? You were saying yourself, I should meet new people, make some new friends. And Jay's a really sweet guy ...' I ran out of breath. 'So, will you take me?'

'No.' Mum pushed away her mug of tea untouched. 'I won't.'

'But, Mum, it's *church*! It's not like it's a bikie gang, they're not drug-dealers!'

'No,' said Mum steadily, but two red spots glowed in her cheeks. 'They're worse than drug-dealers. They'll try to fill your head with lies, and guilt, and damnation. You keep away from them, Bridie. They're dangerous.'

'They're about as dangerous as ... as fairy floss.'

'Fairy floss rots your teeth, and religion rots your brain!' flashed Mum.

Suddenly I was shouting, my face was hot, and tears had sprung into my eyes. 'This is *ridiculous*! They're good people. They were talking about *love*, what's wrong with that? I'm sixteen years old; you can't decide who my friends are. You can't control what I think! It's *not fair*!'

Then Mum was shouting too. 'I don't want you getting mixed up with those people! They might seem sweet and harmless, but it's poison, Bridie, believe me. Bridie, *don't* you turn your back on me. Bridie, don't you dare walk away when I'm speaking. Bridie, I mean it—'

But it was too late. I'd already marched down the hallway, and slammed the front door behind me.

Mish answered my knock. 'Back again? Did you leave something behind?' Then she saw my face, and stepped back to let me in. 'Stella's gone with Paul and Tark to take Nora home; you can wait if you like ...'

'Sorry,' I said, wiping my eyes. 'I just had this stupid fight with Mum, and I ...'

'Oh, well, we've all done that,' said Mish. 'Want to talk about it?'

I followed her into the big room. Scarlet was at the computer; she swivelled round, saw it was me, said, 'Oh, hi,' and went back to what she was doing.

'I only asked her for a lift,' I told Mish. 'The way she carried on, you'd think I was joining the Nazi Party or something.'

'This is about the Christians?'

'I'm not going to *be* one. I'm not joining or anything.'

'Just looking, eh?' Mish put the kettle on. 'Is it because you like this boy Jay?'

'Did Stella say ...?'

Mish shook her head.

'I do like him,' I said. 'But not like *that*.'

'So what's the attraction?'

I wasn't really sure. Part of it was feeling annoyed with Mum and Stella for slagging off Christians. They shrugged aside all the good stuff about them as if it didn't count, as if it didn't mean anything. And there was something about the atmosphere at Northside that had appealed to me – not just Pastor Matt's speech, not just the songs – something about the way everyone had smiled at me, the welcoming, the warmth. It felt safe there, but exciting too – alive, and vibrant, and purposeful. And I wanted to find out more.

I mumbled, 'I just liked it.'

Mish poured boiling water into the teapot. 'Well, like I said, I think it's great that you're exploring your spiritual side. If you need help, I'll help you. I'll drive you to the youth group. This week, anyway. But I'm very unreliable, you shouldn't count on me.'

'Wow, really, Mish? Thanks.'

'But I want you to do something for me. Ask your mum why she's so against religion.'

'Because she's a fascist.'

'Bridie, I'm serious. Ask her, okay?'

'Okay,' I said. But that was one conversation I intended to put off as long as possible. Preferably forever.

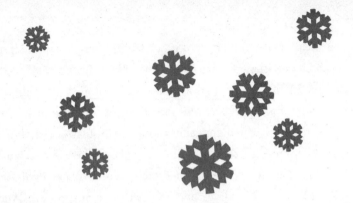

I DIDN'T TELL JAY I was coming. Maybe there was a part of me that suspected I might change my mind at the last minute, and I didn't want to promise, then let him down.

On the other hand, I had no problem lying to my mother. It wasn't *exactly* lying; I told her I 'might' have dinner with the Kincaids on Wednesday. Which I might, if I did pull out at the last minute.

Mum said, 'Oh, good,' in great relief, obviously thinking the crisis was over: my crisis of faith. Only, my crisis was that I might be catching faith instead of losing it. Could you catch faith? Was it infectious?

Even if I did catch it, it didn't have to be fatal. Look at Paul – he'd recovered, and the only side effect he'd suffered was a serious case of being good.

Paul helped heaps of people; he was lovely. Mish said once that he could have worked longer hours and got a job that paid more but he didn't, so he had time to do all the voluntary stuff, and hang out with his family. If he'd had a high-powered job, they could have renovated their house, or bought a bigger one, and sent Stella, Scarlet and Tark to expensive schools. But he didn't. He just wanted to live a good life. Maybe it was God that set him on his good path in the first place; I'd never thought of that before.

If I had a dad, I'd want him to be like Paul. Stella didn't know how lucky she was.


It was Stella who let me in when I turned up for my lift on Wednesday. 'Oh, hi.' There was a slight coolness in her voice. She yelled out, 'Mum! Bridie's here!'

We stood close together in the narrow hallway while noise flowed over us: Scarlet was singing, Tark yelled, the TV was blaring. Mish called, 'Has anyone seen my bloody *keys*?'

I looked at Stella. 'Sure you don't want to come?'

'No, thanks.'

'Are we on for Tim tomorrow morning?'

Was it my imagination, or did she hesitate slightly before she answered? 'Yeah, tomorrow.'

I said in a rush, 'Stell, you know, I'm not going because of Jay. I'm not after him or anything.'

'Whatever. I'm not after him either.'

'That's okay, then.'

'Yep,' said Stella crisply. She stood aside to let Mish past.

Mish looked harassed as she juggled her car keys. 'Keep an eye on those spuds, Stella, I should be back in half an hour or so. Ready, Bridie? How long do you think this thing'll run?'

'Jay said till nine.' I felt awful. My spiritual explorations seemed to be inconvenient for everyone. 'But someone'll give me a lift home.'

'No, no, I'll pick you up. Just because a person belongs to a church, they could still be a child molester.'

'Well, der,' said Stella. '*More* likely, don't you think? Anyway, Mother, Bridie's hardly a *child*.' She rolled her eyes at me, which was a good sign.

As I climbed into the car I said, 'Stella doesn't approve.'

'Stella's anti-school at the moment, which means she's anti-everything.' Mish threw the car into gear and lurched into the road in her usual erratic style. 'Don't worry about it.'

'I don't expect you to do this every week,' I said as we careered down the highway.

'Every *week*?' Mish was silent for a second. 'We'll see.'

I realised Mish didn't expect me to go back after tonight. She thought I'd get it out of my system, see the light, and leave. I felt a surge of the same irritation that flared up whenever Mum or Stella sneered at Northside. They were so smug, so certain they knew better than me. Even Mish, who was supposed to be on my side.

When we arrived, golden light was streaming from the windows of the big, low barn of the church. A group of teenagers spilled from another car and called to a guy in the open doorway, who raised his hand in greeting.

'Sure about this?' said Mish. 'You can still change your mind.'

'No, I'm fine.' I smiled as I unbuckled my seatbelt. 'I've just seen someone I know.'

The guy in the doorway was Elliot. 'Hey, Bridie! Jay told me to watch out for you. Glad you could make it. Come on, I'll take you in.' He put his hand on my shoulder, with his arm almost around me. I shivered, but not from cold.

Gently, Elliot propelled me inside and downstairs into a large basement room full of plastic chairs, bright posters and beanbags and the excited babble of teenagers. Heads turned as we walked in, and everyone smiled and said hi – not just to Elliot, but to me too.

As soon as Jay saw us, he rushed over and seized both my hands and held them, beaming. 'Bridie! It's great to see you!'

Instantly, Elliot lifted his hand from my shoulder. 'Jay will look after you now,' he said, and smiled too; he wasn't scowly at all. 'I have to go and bring in our speaker.' And he vanished back upstairs.

'Wow,' said Jay. 'I can't believe you're here.' He squeezed my hands and gazed into my eyes. I felt my face glowing red, but I couldn't help smiling back. I don't think anyone had ever been so pleased to see me before.

Still holding one of my hands, Jay led me round the room and introduced me to everyone. 'This is Bridie Vandenberg – she saved me from getting beaten up that time.'

'Oh, *yeah*,' they all said. '*Bridie*. Wow.'

It was like being famous; it seemed everyone had heard the story. Ryan, Juliet, Adam, Oliver, Shanelle … I met so many people my head was spinning. And they weren't freaks – just normal kids. Slightly more smiley than average, sure, but how could that be a bad thing? When Elliot brought in the guest speaker, a visiting pastor from another church, Jay led me to a chair and sat down beside me, still holding my hand.

All week I'd told myself that the reason I was coming to this meeting was to hear a debate about the war, but with only one speaker, it wasn't exactly a debate. And even though he talked about the war, he didn't mention politics, or human rights, or the global economy, or any of the reasons other people said the war had started. Instead he spoke about 'the last days'; he seemed to be saying that this war, and wars all over the world, climate change, the drought, and the return of high-waist pants, were all signs that the end of the world was coming. (Okay, I made it up about the high-waist pants.) As though it were all part of some grand but mysterious plan, as though God was preparing us for something. We, sitting in this room, had been chosen by God to play a very special part in this plan; *we* were going to save the world.

I didn't totally understand everything he said, but a weird thrill ran over me when he spoke about us, the young people, being marked out for this special responsibility. And when you thought about it, it made sense: we were going to inherit the world, after all. It was up to us to fix up the mess that past generations had left behind. Previously, I'd found that thought quite overwhelming and depressing, but sitting there with Jay and everyone else, so flushed and excited, I started to believe that maybe we could do it after all. It was sort of the same feeling I'd had at the peace rally, but now the feeling was stronger, more focussed. It was God who would grant us the strength and the courage to take on this fight. As long as we had faith in Jesus, He would take care of us. He'd show us the way. Our job was to be the best we could be, as perfect as we could be, for Him.

Everyone was nodding and murmuring, 'Amen.'

The pastor swept his gaze around the room. 'I can't hear you!'

'Amen! *Hallelujah*!' Some people jumped up and punched the air.

'I can't hear you!'

'AMEN! HALLELUJAH! PRAISE THE LORD!'

Jay jumped up and pulled me with him, and I shouted out too, because everyone else did, and we made such a joyful noise the roof nearly blew off, and suddenly everyone started to sing a song about Jesus coming back.

I whispered to Jay, 'Jesus is coming *back*?'

'Yeah, of course.' Jay grinned at my surprise, and swung my hand. 'The Bible says so.'

'Oh,' I said. 'Okay.'

The song peaked in a crescendo of whoops and applause, and before I knew it, Jay had pulled me into a quick hug, then released me. 'I'll … I'll get us some hot chocolate,' he said, blushing, and dashed off. I was still blinking after him when Elliot came over. He wasn't scowling, but he did look stern. 'Bridie.'

I clutched at the back of my chair; it was really hot in the basement. I tried to think of something to say. 'Elliot,' I blurted. 'Could I ask you something? About Jesus?' That sounded weird, spoken out loud. Probably not so much to Elliot, though. I plunged on. 'You know how Christians talk about Jesus dying for our sins? What does that mean?'

Elliot scratched his chin and rubbed his hand thoughtfully across his forehead. 'We're all sinners, Bridie,' he said. 'We're all stained by sin.'

'What, even little babies?'

'The whole human race. We've all broken God's laws. Sins have to be paid for, sins have to be punished. When Jesus died, He paid for all our sins, forever. So when you accept Christ as your saviour, you're given eternal life.'

'So you go to heaven?'

'More than that. When Jesus returns to rule over the earth forever, you'll live forever with Him.'

'But ... *how* did Jesus pay?'

'With His life, Bridie. He died so that we can live.'

'I don't get it. Why did He have to die?'

'He's the sacrifice. He took the punishment.'

'God's punishment?'

'Yes.'

'So if Jesus hadn't died, we'd all be punished? God would punish us? We'd go to hell?'

'Hell isn't ... some people think hell is an actual place. Some people think hell is the state of being denied God's presence. And heaven is the opposite; it's being in God's presence always. It's the eternal bliss of being with God.'

'Sending us to hell doesn't sound like a very loving thing to do.'

'God is our father, Bridie. Doesn't your father punish you when you do the wrong thing? How else do you learn?'

'I don't have a father.'

There was a pause. 'I'm sorry to hear that, Bridie.'

'Well,' I said awkwardly. 'That's okay.' We looked away from each other; Elliot frowned at the crush around the cake and drink table. I said in a rush, 'Jay seems well.'

Elliot's mouth tightened. 'He isn't.'

'What ... what's happened?'

'We just found out. His eye is permanently damaged. He might lose the sight completely.'

'Oh, God!' Then I realised what I'd said. 'I mean—'

'It's okay.' Elliot scowled across the room. 'That's what I've been saying, too. How could God let this happen? To Jay, of all people.'

'But he seems so ...'

'Oh, he's amazing. He's very forgiving. Much more forgiving than me.' Elliot gave a savage laugh. His gaze roamed around the basement full of happy, excited, young people who could see perfectly, and he looked as though he hated them all. He said quietly, 'I could kill those bastards. And I'm angry with God, for letting them do this to him.'

'Well, that's totally understandable ...'

'The worst thing is, it's my fault. I should have been there taking care of him.' Elliot's voice was low and bitter, and suddenly he looked back at me. 'I shouldn't be telling you all this. Sorry. That's not why you came here.'

I heard myself say, 'Maybe it is.'

And then Jay was bumping my elbow with two hot chocolates and some cake on a plate. When I turned back, Elliot had vanished into the crowd.

'Elliot told me about your eye. I'm really sorry,' I said awkwardly.

He smiled ruefully. 'Yeah, it's a bummer. But I'm not giving up hope. Everyone's praying for me.'

He said it in such a matter-of-fact way. Prayer and the Bible were just an ordinary part of his life, the way, I dunno, talking about politics was part of mine. I remembered Mish saying that she believed in the power of prayer, even if she wasn't sure there was anyone to listen.

I said, 'Should I pray for you, too?'

'Thanks,' said Jay. He touched my hand. 'That'd mean a lot to me.'

I felt my face burn. 'I'm … I'm not sure I believe in God, though.'

Jay looked at me, and the rest of the room, all the noise and talk and laughter, seemed to fall away. He said softly, 'Then what are you doing here, Bridie?'

I whispered, 'I'm not sure.'

Jay's hand tightened around mine, and he bowed his head. 'Almighty Father.' It took me a second to realise what he was doing. 'We thank you for the many gifts you have given us, for good friends and for the grace of your love.' All around us, conversation hushed, people fell silent, heads dropped. I squeezed my eyes shut. Jay continued, quiet, unself-conscious, as if God was standing in the room beside us. 'Father, we thank you for leading Bridie here to us tonight. She is such a special, wonderful person, and a loving friend. We pray that she opens her heart to your love, that she finds your grace. We pray that she comes to know your love just as surely as we do ...'

I should have been embarrassed. I should have felt like an idiot, standing there with a plate of cake in one hand and Jay grasping the other, praying for me, telling a room full of people how special I was.

But strangely, I felt a sense of peace and calm, like a huge, warm, protective hand lowered over us all. And when I raised my head, I saw Elliot, too, with his head bowed and his hands gripped on the back of a chair. His lips were moving.

And for the first time, I was sure there must be *something* there, some power or presence, and that Jay and Elliot knew it, and trusted it, in spite of everything. And it was that conviction that lodged in me that night.

After I got home, I sat by my bedroom window and looked up at the silver moon. For the first time ever in my life, I said silently, *Please, God ...*

It was easier when I closed my eyes. Instantly I felt that same warmth travel down my spine, that sense of waiting stillness. I couldn't pray like Pastor Matt, or even like Jay. So I just said silently, *Please let Jay's eye get better. Please let the war end soon. Let the soldiers be okay. Please watch over the innocent people.* I paused. *Thank you for Jay and Elliot. Please look after them both.* And even though I knew they'd hate it, I added, *Please watch over my mum, and over Stella too. And me*, I added as an afterthought. *Thank you.*

That was where my words ran out, so I opened my eyes and looked out into the dark. And I knew that something, someone, somewhere, had been listening to me, and I felt the most wonderful sense of peace.

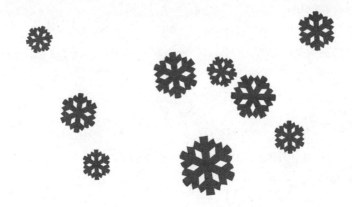

AS SOON AS I woke up in the morning, I knew there was something exciting that I had to remember – and then it came to me. God was real! God was real, and I was going to get to know Him better. The knowledge lay in my heart, solid and radiant as a pearl. And the answer to a question that I hadn't asked presented itself with crystal certainty: I couldn't keep it a secret from Mum any longer. That was a lie, and it was wrong. I would have to tell her.

It was a Tim-and-Stella morning. As we walked, I waited for Stella to ask me about youth group, but she talked about other things – school stuff, her concert, the latest war news – as if she didn't want to know, as if she was determined to pretend it hadn't happened.

But all the time we were walking under the grey and golden sky, I was aware of a kind of glow inside me. As if God were watching me. What did He see? *Oh, God*, I prayed silently. *Let me be the best person I can be; let me be perfect, for You.*

'Hello?' said Stella. 'Are you even listening to me?'

'Sorry,' I said hastily. But I wasn't listening, not really.

Between my conversation with God, and rehearsing the conversation I was going to have with Mum when I got home, I didn't have much attention to spare for Stella.

'Mum.'

'Mm?' She didn't even look up from the paper.

'Mum, I have to tell you,' I took a deep breath, 'that youth group you didn't want me to go to? I went.'

For a second Mum didn't say anything. She pressed her hands flat on the tabletop. Then she murmured something.

'Sorry?'

'I said, *turn it off.*'

Her voice was jerky; I stumbled across the kitchen to switch off the radio, and stayed there, barricading myself behind a chair. There was a long pause. Maybe Mum was counting to ten before she spoke.

'Are you planning to go again?'

'You told me I should make some new friends …'

'Believe me, this is not what I had in mind!'

'What's the big deal?' I said. 'What's your *problem*? Just because *you're* a scientist, *I* can't even *think* about religion? Because you don't believe in God, no one else is allowed to? Why shouldn't I explore my spirituality? Mish thinks it's a great idea.'

Mum snorted. 'Mish *would.*'

Then I remembered. 'Mish said I should ask you why you're so anti-religion.'

Mum's face went white. 'Mish should mind her own business.'

74

Then I lost it. 'You are such a hypocrite! You can't control where I go. You can't control what friends I make, and you *really* can't control what I believe! Why don't you mind *your* own business?'

I stormed down the corridor and slammed my bedroom door. The lovely serenity of the morning had dissolved, like mist off the river. All that was left was hurt and rage. I tried to think, *Dear God* ... But I was too furious to pray.

There was a knock at the door.

'Go away!' I yelled.

'Please, Bridie,' came Mum's muffled voice. 'We need to talk.'

I scuffed my shoes on the floorboards, and then I got up and let her in. I sat on the edge of the bed with my arms folded, staring at the wall.

Mum pulled out my chair and sat down. There was silence.

'Well?' I said at last. 'I'm going to be late for school.'

'You can be late for once,' said Mum. 'This is more important.'

That scared me; Mum had *never* let me be late for school. I sat up straighter. 'Well?' I said again, less angry and more curious.

Mum said, 'I'm going to tell you a story.'

I waited. It took a long time for her to get started.

'Once upon a time, there was a young woman who lived in Brisbane with her parents.'

'And her name was Lisa,' I interrupted. I knew Mum was from Brisbane, that was no great revelation.

Mum closed her eyes and ignored me. 'This young woman

and her parents were members of a church, quite a strict church, called the Children of Jesus.'

My mouth fell open. Back in the depths of my mind, large objects began to clunk into place.

'This young woman had a relationship with a man who didn't belong to the church, and she became pregnant. The Children of Jesus are ... strict. The young woman could have been expelled from the church; her parents, too. Her parents were very shocked and angry and upset. But they came up with a plan. They knew a childless couple, members of their church, who wanted to adopt a baby. The parents decided that their daughter should go away into the country and have her baby and – and give it to this couple.'

My mouth still hung open. 'But you can't *do* that.' My voice squeaked. 'You can't give away a baby like a ... like a puppy!'

'It's hard to believe,' agreed Mum. Her voice was very steady now, as if she really was telling someone else's story; I couldn't get my head around the fact that she was talking about us, about her and me. 'It's like something in a book. But the young woman's parents insisted that she had to give up the baby, or they could never forgive her. They said God would never forgive her. And she told them ...' Mum looked me in the eye. '*I* told them to go to hell.'

I couldn't speak.

'I said I was going to keep my baby, whatever the consequences. So my parents threw me out of the house. They said someone who had entered so deeply into sin and remained unrepentant could no longer be their daughter.'

'They wanted to give me away,' I said wonderingly, 'to strangers; my own grandparents.' I looked at Mum. 'What did you do? What about ...' I hesitated. 'What about my father?'

Mum laughed bitterly. 'He didn't want to know. All *I* knew was that I couldn't lose you. I was young and scared. I ran away, here, to a different city. And I held onto you,' said Mum fiercely. 'And I never let you go.'

I sat frozen. I should have known; I should have guessed. Maybe I hadn't wanted to know. I was always vaguely aware that there was something wrong between Mum and her parents, and that my existence, and my father's non-existence, was probably part of it. But I'd never dreamed that Mum had had to run away to save me. I hadn't known how brave she was, or how cruel and wicked my grandparents had been. It was like a fairytale. I couldn't believe they could just give me away. Like a stray kitten. Useless. Unwanted.

'You never told me,' I said.

Mum ran her fingers through her hair; she looked shattered, as if she'd stayed up all night. 'I didn't want you to hate them,' she said wearily.

'That's why we never see them. It's not because Grandpa's too sick to travel!'

Mum forced a smile. 'It's not as bad as it was. I took you there to meet them once, do you remember?'

'When I was five – and you had those massive arguments.'

'They can't accept that I decided to raise you alone. They can't accept that I don't have a husband. They can't accept that

I've left the church, that I don't believe in their God any more, that I don't need Him.'

'Or them,' I said.

Mum looked surprised. 'Or them,' she repeated, as if she'd never thought of that before.

I said numbly, 'So now it's just – Christmas cards.'

'I did the right thing,' Mum said suddenly. She raised her eyes to me and I saw an expression I'd never seen before, an uncertainty, a vulnerability. It frightened me. Mum was always so sure of herself, so determined, so clear. I always pretended that it bugged me, but deep down I needed her that way. I didn't want to know about Mum's doubts, her mistakes. I had to believe she knew exactly what she was doing. She was my mum; she was all I had; she was the shield that stood between me and the world. I needed her to be stronger than me, wiser, and in control.

'Of course you did the right thing!' I cried, and so I didn't have to see that vulnerability in her face, I threw myself across the room. I hugged her, and she hugged me back hard. We hardly ever hugged any more. I could tell that she was crying. After a minute she gently but firmly pushed me away. Mum hated anyone to see her being emotional, even me.

'Now do you understand why I don't want you mixed up with a church?' she said quietly.

I nodded; I didn't trust myself to speak. But already my mind was busy forming arguments: *Northside isn't like that. They are all about love, and acceptance, and gathering people in. Jay and Elliot and Pastor Matt, Juliet and Adam and Shanelle wouldn't have turned you and me away. Elliot says Jesus has forgiven all our sins, right? And God thinks I'm special, Jay said so. And I can feel it inside, the power of God's love.*

'You'd better get ready for school,' said Mum.

But I lingered in the doorway. 'Mum? About Gran and Grandpa, did you ever... did you ever forgive them?'

'They did what they thought was right,' said Mum wearily. 'For both of us. They meant it for the best. I've thought about this for a long time, and I do believe now, they acted out of love.'

'But can you forgive them?'

Mum didn't say anything; then after a minute she gave her head a quick, violent shake. She said in a low voice, 'Never.'

As I stood in the shower, I thought about God and religion. How could a mother and father throw out their own daughter, reject their own innocent unborn grandchild, just because they believed God thought it was wrong to have sex before you were married? How could anyone be so sure they knew what God wanted, and be so scared of Him, that they'd put the rules of their religion before love of their own child?

I knew Mum's story was supposed to make me doubt God, supposed to put me off Northside. But weirdly, it didn't. Northside's God, the God I'd met last night, couldn't be the same as the God of the Children of Jesus, whoever they were. They'd got it wrong; they'd muddled things up. That was *their* problem. *Our* God, mine and Jay's and Elliot's, wasn't like that.

In fact, in a strange way, knowing about Mum's family made me more convinced than ever that I was *meant* to go to

Northside, meant to know God better. Maybe faith was in my blood, or something.

I imagined telling Stella, 'Now that I know I'm descended from a family of religious freaks, I'm even more curious to observe them up close.'

Even a week ago, I could have said that to Stella, and she'd have laughed. But I wasn't sure she'd find it funny now.

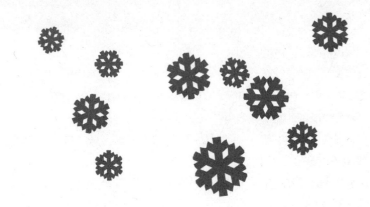

STELLA TEXTED ME on Friday night to see if I could walk Tim on Saturday morning instead of Sunday; Scarlet wanted to swap. I texted back *OK* with a spasm of relief. Because, of course if I went to church on Sunday, I couldn't walk with Stella, and I'd dreaded telling her. I dreaded telling Mum, too; I kept putting it off, and the longer I waited, the worse I felt.

I kept having the same bad dream: I was in the middle of the war, crouching in a ruined house, like the ones on the news every night, while bombs whistled overhead. Explosions shook the ground, more violent each time. Someone was with me, but I couldn't see who. They put their lips close to my ear, and through the whine of the bombs and the explosions, they breathed, 'It's coming ...' And in the dream I felt a rush of wind, as if all the oxygen was sucked from the air, and I knew that this was it, the end.

I'd wake up sweating, my heart banging in my chest. And I'd tell myself it was just a dream, that I was safe.

But the people who lived in the cities under fire, the soldiers on both sides, couldn't wake up. I prayed for them; all over the world, people prayed. But the war didn't stop.

Saturday morning was cold and clear as glass. The river reflected the trees and the empty sky. Stella hurled a stick for Tim and he bounded after it, barking joyfully, almost tripping over his own stumpy legs in his excitement.

'Stell,' I said. 'I've got something to tell you.'

'Yeah?'

'It's about Mum.' And I told her the story of the Children of Jesus, and Grandpa and Gran and Mum and me.

'Wow,' said Stella. 'That's *hardcore*.' She squeezed my arm. 'I hate to say it, but what else would you expect from God-botherers.'

I said, 'Mmm.' Tim brought back the stick and I flung it away again.

'You're not going back to that church, are you? Bridie, you're *kidding* me. Even now you know what they're like?'

'They're not the same people. That was Brisbane. That was sixteen years ago. Northside's not like that.' I almost said, *God's not like that*.

Stella flicked back her hair. 'Just tell me one thing. Are you after Jay, or not?'

'*Not*. I told you already.'

'It's okay if you are. I'm not interested any more.'

'Gee, thanks. So I can have your rejects, can I?'

'That's not what I meant!'

Then I remembered. 'Elliot said the other night that Jay might lose his eye.'

Stella stopped in her tracks. 'Oh no, seriously? God, that's awful. Poor Jay.'

'I thought you didn't care about him any more?'

'I can still be sorry about him going *blind* without wanting to be his girlfriend,' snapped Stella.

'Yeah, okay,' I said after a second. 'Sorry.'

Stella shot me a sidelong glance. 'So if you're not in love with Jay … you're not in love with *Jesus*, are you?'

'I hardly know Jesus,' I said uncomfortably. Though it was true, I wanted to get to know Him better. Jay talked about Jesus as if He was a real person, as if He was still around, someone he could to talk to any time. I didn't feel like that yet, but I was starting to wish I did. It sounded so comforting – and exciting too, to have a direct connection with this amazing, loving person.

Stella's voice broke in on my thoughts. 'I don't get it.'

'Get what?'

'How people can just believe whatever the priest or whoever tells them. It's all about being told what to think, not thinking for yourself. It's in the Bible – well then, it must be true.' She gave a sarcastic snort. 'Have they actually *read* the Bible? Have you?'

'Bits of it,' I said.

'Yeah? Have you found the part where it says you should be put to death for working on the Sabbath, or being rude to your parents? Or the part that forbids you to wear clothes made out of two different kinds of cloth? It's all in there. These people just pick out the bits that suit them and ignore the bits that don't. When it's about condemning gay people, then it's God's word and we have to obey. But I bet Pastor Matt never preaches about giving all his money away, or throwing the shopkeepers out of the temple, does he?'

'How would you know?' I said, my temper rising. 'It's easy for you to stand there and abuse them, but you don't know anything about it!'

'Oh, I know.' Stella threw the stick into the middle of the oval and Tim raced away. 'You're too smart for all this, Bridie. Church is for thick people, people who want to be told what to think. Lisa was smart enough to get out; you should be smart enough not to join in the first place.'

'I will decide for *myself*,' I said. 'And that means I won't stop going just because you and Mum tell me to. No one from Northside's forcing me into anything. *You're* the only people trying to tell me what to think.'

Stella backed off. 'No, I'm not.'

'Oh, really?' I jammed my hands into my pockets.

Stella whistled for Tim and we walked on in silence. When we'd crossed the second bridge, Stella said, 'Coming back for breakfast?'

I shook my head. 'Got an essay to write.'

'Oh. Okay.' Stella swished Tim's stick in the damp grass. 'Tuesday morning, then?'

'Yeah.'

She didn't ask me if I was going to Northside tomorrow. I guess it was pretty clear that I was. The more Stella and Mum tried to talk me out of getting to know God, the more determined I was to keep on exploring Him for myself. If God really had chosen me, that was more important than what Stella or Mum thought. This could be the most important thing that ever happened to me. I couldn't just walk away – not even for them.

The next morning, I caught the train to Northside by myself. Mum was still in bed when I left, so I didn't have to explain to her, though I wasn't looking forward to that conversation when I got home.

As soon as I arrived, Chelsea came up and started chatting, and then Jay came over. We all sat together with Adam and Ryan and Shanelle and the others, and we clapped and sang and prayed together.

It was as if Pastor Matt knew exactly what I'd been going through. He spoke about the difficult, unfashionable path of following Christ. He said we should try to understand those who jeered or attacked us, because deep down they were afraid of the truth. They were afraid to take the leap that we had taken, to leave their old lives behind. But we should stretch out our hands to them and encourage them to make the leap too, and they would find, just as we had, that they could fly.

A light went on inside my head. Of course Stella was angry with me. I'd always been her faithful shadow; we'd done everything together; I'd let her lead me everywhere. Now for the first time, I was striking out on my own. Of course she was angry; she was jealous! She was scared God would take me away from her.

And I understood Mum. She wanted to believe that her parents loved her, that they'd acted out of love. So she blamed the church for what her parents had done. She needed to believe that it wasn't their fault.

Christianity was for thick people, was it, Stella? I felt pretty wise this morning, buoyed with joy, my new friends on either side and the warmth of God's blessing upon me. And when Pastor Matt prayed, I prayed for Mum and Stella, and I forgave them. A glow bloomed inside me, solemn and large, brave and defiant and noble.

It turned out Chelsea and her mum Lorraine lived not far from my place, so they gave me a lift home. Lorraine said she'd drive me every week if I liked, and to youth group, too. And I thought how wrong Stella was about these people, how nice and friendly and *good* they were. And now I was one of them, and I was proud.

When I got home, Mum was doing the Sunday crossword.

'Were you at the Kincaids?' she said, and I think she would have preferred it if I'd lied and said yes, but I stood straight and tall and told the truth.

Armed with my new courage, my new understanding, I let the waves of her anger break over me. I didn't fight back, and at last Mum ran out of energy. She couldn't break me; she couldn't defeat the power of God's love. At last she sank onto the couch and gazed at me with a kind of bewilderment.

'Are you even listening to me?'

'Yes, Mum.' *I forgive you.*

Her shoulders sagged. 'You know how I feel. I don't want to go on having this argument.'

'No, Mum.' I braced myself for the next round. But it seemed that Mum had nothing more to say. I stared, amazed that it was so easy. It was true, with God on your side, anything was possible. I felt a lump in my throat. 'I love you, Mum.'

She looked up sharply in case I was making fun of her; but I was totally sincere. With an effort she said, 'I love you, too.'

'Can I go now?'

Mum opened her mouth, then she sighed and shrugged, and I escaped to my room. I could hardly wait to pray, to give my thanks.


It rained overnight, and on Tuesday morning the twigs of the bare trees were beaded with water. Stella whacked a branch with a stick, and rain splattered over us.

'You go to church on Sunday?'

'Yep.'

Stella nodded. I was all prepared to defend myself, and to forgive her, too, but she didn't give me a chance. Instead she said abruptly, 'I had the *worst* day yesterday.'

'What happened?'

'I'm in big trouble.' There was a certain satisfaction in her voice, as if she'd been planning this for a while. 'And it's kind of your fault.'

'*My* fault?'

'You got me thinking about this stuff.' She threw back her hair. 'At St Marg's, every Monday there's an assembly for the whole school, and they like the seniors to give talks. It might be about a charity in Africa, or someone might read an inspirational poem, or talk about a saint or something.' Stella pulled a face. 'So yesterday I got up and I talked about Why I Am an Atheist.'

I gave a gasp of laughter. '*Stella!*'

'Are you offended?' Stella walked backward to scrutinise my face. 'I was scared to tell you, now that you're a God-botherer.'

I didn't believe that; my guess was that Stella thought up this whole stunt specifically to shock me – and St Marg's, of course. And then when I was offended, she could say I was one of those daggy, humourless Christians who couldn't take a joke. 'That was cheeky,' I said mildly.

Stella looked slightly disappointed. 'Yeah, it was. Everyone was so paralysed with shock that I finished the whole speech before someone dragged me off. Then it was straight to Miss Bernard's office; I was there for *hours*.'

We paused while Stella picked up Tim's poo and tied the bag. She said, 'Nana reckons I wouldn't have done it if you were around. She said "Bridie would have talked you out of it. Bridie always keeps you under control."'

I was startled. I'd thought a lot about what *I'd* lost when Stella changed schools, but not so much about what *Stella* might have lost.

'So did they give you detention, or what?' I asked.

'Oh, no, they don't do detention at St Marg's; it's all about "Restorative Resolution". Today I'm supposed to apologise to the whole school for not taking their faith seriously.' Stella rolled her eyes. 'Bernie said she wouldn't have minded if she thought I was sincere, but she was really cross because I was only stirring.'

*Bernie knows Stella pretty well*, I thought. 'And were you?'

Stella shrugged. 'Bit of both. Anyway, they can shove their apology. What's the worst they can do, expel me? I wish they would!'

'Is that why you did it?' I stopped in the middle of the path, and a cyclist dinged his bell and swooped impatiently around us.

'It's not about *you*, if that's what you're thinking.'

'Isn't it?'

'You're not the centre of my universe, Bridie Vandenberg.'

'You're jealous, because I've found something new, something of my own, new friends.'

'I don't *think* so. Do you mean your new invisible friend Jesus? Or that pack of brain-dead zombie Christians? I wouldn't hang out with *them* if you paid me.'

'That is the dumbest generalisation I ever heard. If they were gay or – or black or Muslim, you wouldn't say that. But because they're Christians, it's okay to *vilify* them?'

Stella tossed back her hair. 'Seriously, Bridie, if you turn into a Christian, I don't think I can be your friend any more.'

Tim pointed his little sharp snout up at me and barked anxiously; he knew there was trouble.

'Well, it's unfortunate you feel like that,' I said coldly. 'Because I *am* a Christian.'

Stella's face was white in the early sunlight. 'You're choosing *them* over me?'

'I'm choosing God,' I said. 'How you feel about it is up to you.'

We stared at each other. And I turned around and crossed back over the bridge. I went home the way we'd come, and left her to finish the circuit on her own.

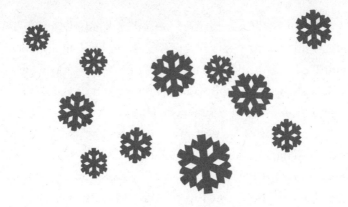

FOR THE NEXT few weeks, I lived like a double agent. The two halves of my existence didn't touch each other.

On Sunday mornings and Wednesday nights, I was a Northsider; the rest of the week, at school and at home, I never mentioned it. But more and more, Northside felt like the place my real life happened. It was the place I could relax, the only place I could talk about God, the place my soul felt free. The only people who truly understood the importance of that belonged to Northside, and now I belonged there, too.

Mum and I never discussed my absences. There was a tense church-shaped gulf between us, but we both acted like if we ignored it for long enough, it would eventually go away.

I didn't turn up to walk Tim any more, and Stella didn't ring or text me, so that was that. For a long time I expected her to make a move. It hurt that she could throw away all our years of friendship – I almost said over something so trivial but it wasn't trivial at all. What to believe, who to believe in, the kind of person you want to be: nothing's more important than that.

Without Stella, there were no other Kincaids in my life either: no chaotic weekend breakfasts, no football arguments with Tark, no helping Scarlet with her homework, no yoga with Mish, no jokes with Paul. In a funny sort of way, I almost missed them as much as I missed Stella herself.

I spent a lot of time in my room, reading the Bible. Jay had given me one, and everyone at Northside assured me that there was no better way to find out about God than to read His Word; so I'd decided to read the whole thing from start to finish. I hated to admit it, but Stella was right: it was pretty confusing. Even in the first two pages of Genesis there were two contradictory creation stories, and Leviticus was full of weird rules about sacrifices and diseases. God didn't come across too well either. He didn't seem loving at all, to tell the truth, always ordering people to kill their first-born sons, and smiting them with plagues and destruction.

I told Elliot I was struggling with the Old Testament, and he advised me to go straight to the New, which was a lot more enjoyable. Jesus was a pretty incredible guy; no wonder they built a whole religion round Him. Some of the things He said gave me chills all over.

'It's amazing,' I said to Jay. 'How His friends were able to write down everything that happened, and it's lasted two thousand years.'

Elliot overheard. 'Actually, Bridie, it wasn't Jesus' friends who wrote the Gospels. The earliest one wasn't written till forty years after His death, and the others were much later. That's why they don't agree on the details.'

'Oh,' I said. 'So – some of it's made up?'

'No,' said Jay firmly. 'It's all true. That's not what Elliot meant, was it, Elliot?'

There was a pause, then 'Yes,' said Elliot vaguely, and he scratched his chin and walked away; I didn't know what to think.


One night in late July, Mum said casually over dinner, 'I've been asked to speak at a public forum at uni in a couple of weeks. Want to come?'

I grimaced. 'Is it about biology?'

'Not just biology, there'll be other speakers too.'

'What's it about?' I spoke through a mouthful of rice.

Mum pushed a flyer across the table. 'Maybe Stella would like to come, too?'

'Stella would come and hear you read a shopping list,' I said absently, turning over the pamphlet. Then I realised that meant Mum would expect me to invite her. I hadn't told Mum about our epic fight, but she's not an idiot; she must have noticed Stella and I weren't exactly best buddies any more. Was this Mum's not-so-subtle attempt to bring us back together? I was still waiting for Stella to apologise. I pushed the problem away as I focussed on the flyer.

*God vs Science*

*'Creation Science' Is Not Science!*

*'Intelligent Design' Is Not Intelligent!*

*Hear the truth about evolution, education and the curriculum conspiracy!*

Then a list of four speakers, including Dr Lisa Vandenberg, and the details of when and where.

'You haven't organised this forum for my benefit, have you?' It was the first time I'd risked a church-based joke, however tiny, with Mum.

Mum took back the flyer. 'No, it's a coincidence.'

I stabbed a beef strip. 'Is anyone talking from the other side?'

'The *other side* have plenty of forums of their own,' Mum said sharply. 'There's no need for the university to give them a public platform.'

'I thought universities were supposed to encourage open debate, the battle of ideas, that kind of thing?'

'When two ideas have equal intellectual value—' Mum stopped herself, and took a deep breath. 'I would really like you to come.'

I pushed rice around my plate. 'I guess I *might*.'

Mum nodded. 'You know, Bridie,' she said. 'At some point, you're going to have to make a choice.'

'It's not on a Northside night, is it?' I figured calling it 'Northside' was less confrontational than 'church'.

'That isn't what I meant.' Mum's face was still and tight.

I chewed my meat, which had taken on the texture of a rubber band. Why would I have to choose? I could go to Northside *and* the evolution forum. I could believe in everything, like Mish. Why did it have to be one or the other?

It wasn't long before I found out why. The next night, to be precise.

'Exciting news, people!' announced Ryan, another of the youth leaders. He brandished one of the forum flyers that Mum had brought home. My stomach lurched. 'A great opportunity! We're going to hold a protest at the university.'

Soon everyone was buzzing with plans: brainstorming ideas for placards and chants, dressing up in monkey suits, that kind of thing.

I'd suspected that creationism might be something that Northside Church was into, but I hadn't realised how fervently they embraced it. I didn't say anything, but as the evening passed I became more and more uncomfortable. This must have been how Stella had felt at church, surrounded by people who believed in stuff she just couldn't swallow.

Because I just couldn't swallow creationism. Maybe it came from having a biologist for a mother, but the idea that God made the earth and everything on it in six days was something I found literally unbelievable.

As usual, Jay was sitting next to me. In the alternative universe that was Northside, we were seen as a couple, even though we'd never done any of the things a normal boyfriend and girlfriend do: never kissed, never been anywhere together except church, never talked about being a couple. But we sat together, and sometimes we held hands. In the eyes of Northside, that seemed to be enough. I wasn't totally comfortable with it, but because we never *did* anything, I allowed it to drift on. I certainly didn't think of Jay as my boyfriend. I wasn't sure if he thought I was his girlfriend. But it was reassuring to know that I could rely on him to keep my seat, that he'd always be there.

He'd acquired a proper black pirate's eye-patch now, and his hair flopped over it rakishly. Sometimes I called him Cap'n Jay. 'You're very quiet tonight,' he said.

'Do you really want to go to another protest, after last time?'

'Can't give up the fight,' he said cheerfully.

'It's not the same fight.'

'We're still doing the Lord's work.' He tried to take my hand but I withdrew it. Usually I enjoyed the safety and security of having Jay beside me, but tonight I felt a bit smothered. Jay's relentless cheeriness seemed … unnatural. How could he bounce back so easily, and put his hand up to risk getting hurt again? Wouldn't a normal person have *some* doubts, some fear?

I didn't want to have mean thoughts about Jay; he didn't deserve it. He genuinely was brave; he was cheerful; his faith was strong. I was a bad person. I said hastily, 'What's with the monkey suit?'

'It's a joke. No way are human beings descended from monkeys.'

'But that's not what evolution says. The theory is that humans and apes have a common ancestry. That's not the same thing.'

Ryan overheard me. 'The so-called theory of evolution is full of holes, Bridie. Even the scientists themselves admit it doesn't explain everything. The complexity of an eye, for example.' That wasn't very tactful, with Jay right there, but Ryan ploughed blithely on. 'The eye is a miracle of engineering. How could that just "evolve" by chance?' He made quote marks in the air. 'It must have been designed. Even the scientists admit that evolution is just a theory.'

'Every scientific explanation is a theory,' I said. 'Every theory is tested. That doesn't mean it's not true. And natural selection *can* explain the development of the eye. It didn't spring up out of nowhere; there are creatures with less complex eyes than ours, with light-sensitive patches on their skin.' I stopped. Everyone in the room had fallen quiet, and they were all staring at me.

Elliot said, 'You seem to know a lot about it, Bridie.'

'My mother's a biologist,' I said miserably. 'She's one of the speakers at this forum, actually.'

'Lisa Vandenberg? Really? She's your mum?' Elliot was animated. 'She lectured me last year in History and Philosophy of Science.'

'Yeah?' I managed to say. What was wrong with me? With Stella and Mum, I'd stuck up for God, and all that had achieved was to make them both angry. But when I was with the God-lovers, I took the side of the non-believers. Did I want *everyone* to hate me?

Chelsea clasped her hands together. 'Oh, wow. You are so lucky. What a wonderful opportunity to bear witness. In front of your own mother!'

'That's great, Bridie.' Jay's face was shining. 'You can show your mum you're not afraid to stand up for the truth.'

I felt like the situation was spiralling out of control. 'But I—'

Elliot rescued me. 'Come on, guys. Bridie's still new to the path. Let's not ask her to do too much at once.'

He sent me a swift glance that no one else saw; he seemed to know how I felt.

'Hey, why shouldn't Bridie bear witness?' Ryan frowned at Elliot. 'No need to spread the negative attitude around.' He turned back to me. 'I've got some stuff you can read about intelligent design. It demolishes all the so-called scientific arguments.'

'Oh … thanks,' I said feebly, and Ryan went off to find the booklets for me, with one last warning glance at Elliot.

'But you will come to the forum?' Jay's keen eye gleamed at me. 'You know what this is? This is a test. God sets us all tests to see how strong we are in the faith, and this is yours.'

'So, no pressure, then?' I said. But Elliot was the only one who smiled.

At the end of the meeting, Ryan led us in prayer. He prayed for our soldiers and their families. I waited for him to pray for the soldiers on the other side, too, and the innocent civilians caught up in the fighting, but he didn't. 'Father, we pray for a quick victory in this war, this war between Christianity and the darkness of false belief. We pray for the overthrow of dictators who suppress Your word. We pray for the defeat of Your enemies.'

I was so shocked I sat rigid, scarcely able to breathe. Ryan made it sound like we should *support* the war! But no one else was horrified; only me. At the end of the prayer I couldn't even echo 'Amen' with everyone else.

When Chelsea came up to apologise because they couldn't give me a lift home, I hardly registered what she said.

'Are you going to call your mum?' Jay prompted me.

I looked at him blankly.

Jay squeezed my arm. 'You okay? You've been weird all night.'

'Um … just school stuff,' I said, turning away from his concerned face, his green-gold eye peering into mine like a searchlight. Suddenly all I wanted was to get out of there.

Elliot appeared, jangling his keys. 'Heard you're short of a lift, Bridie. I can drop you home.'

'I'll come too,' Jay said.

'No need,' said Elliot. 'You can go with Ryan.'

Jay's face fell. 'Yeah, okay. See you on Sunday, Bridie.'

'Okay,' I said, but my smile felt plastered to my face. Elliot steered me toward his car. The doors clunked shut and locked us into a space of blessed silence.

Elliot didn't speak until we were speeding down the highway. 'Pretty full on, tonight, hey.'

I gave him a cautious sideways glance. His face was stern in profile, lit by the passing streetlights. He'd started to grow a reddish beard; it didn't suit him.

'Ryan's prayer,' I said. 'I didn't know Northside was pro-war.'

Elliot frowned. 'I wouldn't say that. No one *wants* war, of course not. But you could argue that it's a good idea to kick out cruel, oppressive tyrants who lock up and murder Christians.'

'But Jay was at the rally; he marched for peace; he got beaten up!'

'Jay was there on his own, it was nothing to do with church.

He was beaten up by anti-war protesters, Bridie. People from your side, students probably, like the police said. They must have seen his placard and got the wrong idea, just like you. They thought he was pro-war.'

'What did his placard say?'

'Jesus loves our soldiers.'

All this time I'd assumed Jay and I were on the same side, that it was skinheads, pro-war marchers, who had attacked him. And maybe he wasn't exactly *for* the war, but it seemed he wasn't exactly against it, either. I covered my mouth with my hand.

Without warning, Elliot swerved the car and pulled over to the side of the road. He turned off the engine and swung around to face me.

'I wasn't there,' he said abruptly. 'He asked me to go with him, and I said no. I knew this might happen. I knew people would think he was supporting the war. I didn't want to be … tainted. But I should have been there. I should have been looking after him. He's my little brother, you know? I let him down.'

'It wasn't your fault,' I said. 'You couldn't know what would happen.'

'The stupid thing is, I do think Jesus loves our soldiers. But I think He loves the other side's soldiers too.'

'Even if they don't believe in Him?'

'For sure. Look, if God's real – if God's love is real – He can't have favourites.'

'*If* God's real?' I said in a small voice.

Elliot let out a deep breath, and looked away. 'Sometimes … sometimes I wonder, these days.'

There was a pause while cars flashed past us.

'You're not too sold on the creation thing either, are you?' I said.

'I don't know, Bridie. Your mum gave me a lot to think about in those lectures last year. I believe God created the universe. But not in six days! I know my Bible, I could practically recite the whole Book of Genesis to you right here and now. But it's *poetry*, yeah? It's symbolic, a myth, a beautiful story. It's the spirit of it that's important, not taking every single word literally. But Dad says—' Elliot fell silent, clearly not wanting to say anything disloyal about Pastor Matt. 'I shouldn't be talking to you like this,' he said softly. 'I'm supposed to help you overcome your doubts, not tell you mine.'

'It's like we're in the same place,' I said. 'We're both on the edge of believing – only you're inside looking out, and I'm outside looking in.'

Elliot breathed a soft, surprised laugh. 'Yeah. That's exactly right. Fringe dwellers of the faith, that's us.' He turned his head, trying to see my face in the dim light. 'Bridie, are you and my brother …?'

'No,' I said at once. 'No, we're just friends.'

Elliot shifted in his seat. He leaned in my direction and, with a shock like electricity, I knew, I just knew he was going to kiss me. I twisted my body towards him, but the seatbelt caught and held me. For a split second we were stupidly frozen, straining toward each other. And then Elliot pulled back and turned away. He didn't look at me.

'Better get you home,' he said, and twisted the key in the ignition.

I stared straight ahead without seeing the road, my heart thumping. When we reached my suburb, Elliot asked for directions, and I felt a fizz of disappointment that he couldn't remember where I lived.

He stopped the car outside my house. I could hardly breathe, wondering if he was going to try to kiss me again, but he stayed locked in his seat, hands clamped to the wheel.

'If you ever want to talk, you know, you can ring me,' I said.

Elliot's eyebrows shot up. 'That's what I'm supposed to say to you. I'm the youth leader.'

'Well, you need someone to talk to, too.'

'Yeah.' He looked straight ahead, and repeated it softly. 'Yeah. Thanks, Bridie.'

I watched him drive away. The tail-lights vanished round the corner, and he was gone. The street was empty, and I felt empty too. I fumbled in my bag for my key, and let myself inside.

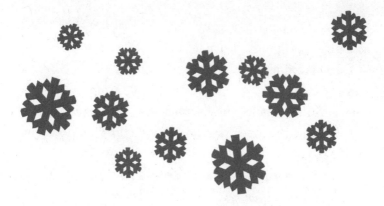

FOR THE NEXT couple of days I moved around in a kind of muddled haze. *You'll have to make a choice*, Mum had said. I hadn't wanted to believe her, but now I had too many choices to make.

Overnight, Northside had stopped feeling like home. They thought the war might be a good thing; they rejected evolution. I always rolled my eyes when Mum raved on about science. I made out I wasn't interested, but it seemed that science had seeped into my bones. It was part of who I was. I couldn't deny it. But would they let me belong to Northside if I didn't deny it? Had Stella been right all along?

And as for the war, even Elliot seemed to think that it might be worth killing thousands of people and destroying cities, to throw out a bad government. But I couldn't bring myself to believe that, and I couldn't believe that God wanted it, either. There had to be a better way.

I imagined arguing about it with Elliot. In fact, I couldn't stop thinking about Elliot, about that moment in the car when he'd leaned toward me. At school, on the bus, in bed at night,

I dreamed that the moment continued, that his arms folded round me, his lips brushed mine, then crushed against them.

I tormented myself wondering if I should tell Jay. But tell him what? It wasn't like anything actually happened; maybe I imagined the whole thing. And it wasn't as if anything had ever happened between me and Jay, either. I didn't owe him anything. Did I?

I knelt in my bedroom and tried to pray. *Dear God, give me a sign. Does Elliot like me?* But I disgusted myself. Surely Almighty God had better things to do than send down a lightning bolt to help me with my teenage crush. You can't ask God to perform party tricks.

I opened my Bible at random and scanned the pages for a message. But it only offered disconnected words like *May this water enter your stomach and cause it to swell up*, or *The second beast looked like a bear standing on its hind legs*. So much for seeking guidance from the Word of God. I knew there was wisdom in these pages, but it was muffled by so much static I couldn't hear it.

I felt like I was losing God. He was withdrawing behind the curtain. Maybe it was Northside I had believed in all along, rather than God. But now I'd lost my faith in Northside, I didn't know where else to look for Him.

I couldn't go back to the way I was before; I couldn't pretend that God wasn't there. He wouldn't let me. I knew He wanted to be part of my life, and I wanted to be part of Him. I just wasn't sure how to do it any more.

Maybe it wasn't God that was lost, maybe it was me.

I couldn't decide what to do about the forum, whether to go and hear Mum speak, which meant inviting Stella, or to stand outside with the Northsiders and their monkey suits. Not going at all would be just a big wuss-out.

On Saturday I was sitting in my room worrying about it, pretending to study but actually flicking through the Bible, when my phone rang.

'Hi, Bridie. It's Elliot.'

I froze. 'Hi!'

I waited for him to speak, but he stayed silent. An explosion of happiness went off in my chest; of all the people in the world, he was the only one who might possibly understand how I was feeling. It was like a sign, the sign I'd asked for.

I clutched the phone to my ear. 'I'm so glad you called! I really need to talk to someone. I'm so confused, I don't know if I can go back to church or not. I mean, I *want* to. I still want God in my life, you know? It's just I'm not sure if— Elliot? Are you still there?'

There was a pause, then Elliot said, 'Bridie, I'm sorry, but I don't think I'm the best person to talk to you about this right now.'

'Okay,' I said uncertainly. 'How come?'

Elliot took a deep breath. 'I'm not ... I've decided I can't be a youth leader any more. I don't feel very strong in the faith at the moment.'

'Right,' I said slowly. 'Does that mean you've stopped believing in God?'

'No, no.' A pause. 'I don't know what I believe, Bridie.' Elliot was quiet, and I could picture him rubbing his hand across his forehead the way he always did. 'There's Jay, his eye ... Since I started uni, I've met people ... Not everyone thinks the same, you know? And that doesn't mean they're evil; it doesn't mean they're stupid. I'm starting to realise, there are other ways to live. Maybe Jesus doesn't have all the answers, after all. Maybe *Dad* doesn't have all the answers. The other night, when we were talking ...' His voice trailed away. 'Listen, Bridie. You're a great person. Just don't ... don't rush into anything, okay?'

I gripped the phone. I didn't know what to say. The ground seemed to shift under me. I hadn't realised how important Elliot's faith was to me. Even if the rest of Northside had revealed themselves to be, well, not as perfect as I'd hoped, I thought I could count on Elliot. I knew he was asking questions, but I assumed that underneath, his faith was solid. It was as if Jesus was a dazzling friend Jay and Elliot had introduced to me, and now Elliot had turned around and said, *No, sorry, I don't trust him.* If Elliot, who'd belonged to the church all his life, could walk away, was there any reason for me to stay? If Elliot didn't believe in God, could I?

'Are you okay?' I asked.

'Um ... not really. But thanks for letting me talk. There's no one else. My uni friends don't get it, you know? And everyone at Northside – they just tell me to get over it, not to be negative.'

'Yeah. I know.' I pressed the phone to my ear. I was about to ask, *Do you want to meet for a coffee or something?* I'd taken a breath to say it. We were fellow fringe dwellers of the faith, weren't we? He'd said so himself.

But then Elliot said abruptly, 'Anyway, thanks. I'll see you round, yeah?'

'Yeah,' I said in a small voice. But he'd already gone.

Next morning when Lorraine knocked at the door, I peeped out at her. 'I can't come to church today. I'm really sorry. I don't feel very well.'

'Oh, no.' Lorraine peered through the crack. 'What's wrong? Anything I can do?'

'Just a bit fluey. Don't want to give it to everyone.'

Lorraine edged forward as if she were about to force her way in. 'You don't *look* sick.'

'Well, I feel like shit,' I said, more sharply than I intended, and Loraine jumped back as if I'd slapped her. The church kids never swore. The church kids never told lies either, at least, none I knew about. That was two sins right there, and on the Sabbath, too.

Lorraine sniffed and turned away. 'Hope you get better. I'll ask Pastor Matt to add you to our prayers.'

'Thanks!' I called after her. Chelsea waved from the car and I waved back. I wondered if Jay would miss me, and felt a twinge of guilt. I'd sort out Jay later.

Mum stepped into the hallway in her dressing-gown. She must have been listening, spying on me. 'Not going to church today?'

'Does it look like I'm going to church?' I snapped. I felt bad enough already, without Mum sticking her nose in.

But she didn't seem to register my tone. 'Oh, thank *God*. I knew you'd come to your senses eventually.' She held out her hand. 'It was partly my fault, I know. I suppose you've been looking for some kind of father figure.'

I stepped back. 'No, I haven't.'

'Well, it doesn't matter. Now that phase is over—'

'Who says it's over?'

Mum wrapped her dressing-gown more tightly round herself. 'You just said you weren't going back!'

'I said I wasn't going *today*. I didn't say I was *never* going back.'

'Bridie, be reasonable. You must see how silly—'

'I'm not going to your stupid evolution forum, either. You can't force me to think like you. You can't take over my brain.'

'That's a *ridiculous* thing to say.'

'Just leave me alone!'

'How *dare* you speak to me like that?'

I can't remember exactly what we said next, or rather, what we shouted at each other. In the end, Mum's expression froze stony cold, and she slammed her bedroom door in my face. I yelled at her, and then marched out of the house and down the street, choking down sobs of rage and fury.

I strode along so fast I gave myself a stitch. I didn't even know where I was going; I only knew I couldn't go back.

At Northside they told us, *You're never alone. Jesus is always with you.* Jay said that Jesus was his friend, always there to listen and to help him. Like Stella said, an invisible friend; an imaginary friend? I'd never quite managed to achieve that sense of Jesus being in the room with me that the other Northsiders seemed to have. They'd sway in ecstasy, holding up their hands to Jesus. Strangely enough, I found it easier to believe in God – a mysterious, unknowable spirit – than in the living person of Jesus.

*Hello, Jesus?* I thought experimentally. *Are you there?*

No answer. Maybe he was off with his mates: the tooth fairy and the Easter bunny.

That was a wicked, blasphemous thought, I told myself. But God didn't strike me down.

How rapt would Mum be if she knew I was having thoughts like that? I sped up, my runners smacking on the footpath.

Once, when I was a little kid, I'd overheard Mum talking about me to one of her friends. *Bridie's a follower*, she said. *Bridie's always looking for someone to tag along behind*. I hadn't thought about that for ages, but I remembered it now. Since I started high school, I guess I'd tagged behind Stella. This winter I guess I'd hung off Elliot and Jay. Was Jesus one more figure for me to trail behind, someone else to tell me what to do?

I crossed the bridge and followed the path beside the river. People were walking their dogs, riding bikes, plugged into iPods. I hadn't been down there for weeks. The river was alive this morning, foaming and tumbling over the weir. A light rain sprinkled. The low morning sun caught the tiny droplets, and the air filled with dancing specks of gold.

The news from the war was bad. The invasion force had met unexpected resistance, fighting in the streets. Last night there was footage on TV of a little boy with his arms and legs blown off, his big eyes glazed with shock and terror. Was he being punished for his sins? If he died, would he go to hell? It seemed he was the wrong religion; he hadn't accepted Jesus as his saviour, that's for sure. How could I believe in a God who was cruel enough to let that little boy feel so much pain and fear?

I crossed halfway over the next bridge and leaned on the rail, staring down into the murky brown water.

'Hey, Bridie!'

I jumped. It was Paul, on the far side of the bridge. He waved, and jogged over to lean on the rail beside me, wiping sweat from his forehead. 'Long time, no see.'

I felt shy. 'Um, yeah.'

'You girls had a fight?'

'Kind of.'

''Bout time you made it up, don't you think?' He squinted at me sideways.

'S'pose,' I mumbled.

A woman jogged past us and the bridge wobbled and swayed. We stood there for a minute while Paul caught his breath.

'Paul?' I said suddenly.

'Shoot.'

'I know you're not in the church, but do you believe in God?'

'Starting with the easy ones, eh?' Paul stared down along the river. 'I wish I could, Bridie,' he said at last, wistfully. 'I just can't quite force my head around it, you know? But I'll tell you what, I believe in *this*.'

He swept his arm out, across the trees dancing in the sunlight, across the cool brown water of the river, the church spires and mosque minarets poking into the sky from the hilltops; across the silver towers of the city beneath the scudding clouds and the transparent circle of the moon; across the suburban rooftops and all the people sheltered beneath them. A flock of birds rose and swooped over the river, calling high and wild and sweet.

Paul turned to me. 'Can't this old world be enough?' he said.

I looked, and I saw that it was beautiful – that the world was full of wonders and mysteries and hope and love and work to be done. All of that was just as real as the fear and suffering and loneliness and cruelty. And I wanted it to be enough; everything would be so simple, if this old world was enough.

But somehow, for me, it wasn't. Something in me yearned for something bigger, something *more*, something beyond what we could see and comprehend. I didn't know what it was, but there had to be more.

I looked at Paul, and I shook my head.

He put his big warm hand on my shoulder. He smelled of sweat. For a second I thought he was going to laugh at me, but he didn't.

'I had a big fight with Mum this morning,' I said.

'You duffer,' said Paul. 'Want to come back to our place?'

I hesitated.

'Come on,' said Paul. 'Think of all the times Stella's run away to your house. We owe you.'

'Stella won't—'

'Don't be daft. She misses you.'

My heart leapt. 'I miss her, too.'

Paul inclined his head. 'So what are you waiting for?'

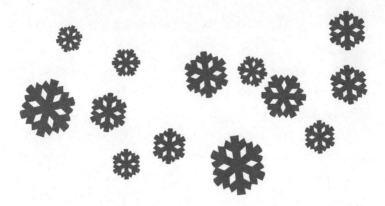

'OF COURSE, YOU can stay as long as you like,' said Mish at once, and Scarlet clapped her hands.

'Can she sleep on our floor?'

Stella pushed her sister. 'Der, where else could she sleep?'

I smiled. I was still shy with Stella, but she did seem pleased that I was there.

'There's plenty of space at my house, Bridie,' Nana Kincaid said. 'Lovely big spare room all to yourself.'

'Thanks,' I said. 'But ...'

Tark lolled against his grandmother. 'As if Bridie wants to stay with a crusty old bat like you.'

'Cheeky,' said Nana. She always let Tark get away with murder.

'Just one thing.' Mish held up a finger. 'You have to call Lisa and tell her where you are. Or would you rather I did?'

'I'd rather you did,' I mumbled.

'Hmm.' Mish narrowed her eyes. 'All right.'

She took the phone into the front bedroom and stayed there a long time. When she came out, her face was grave, but she didn't say anything. Much later, after Nana had gone home, when Paul was off on some refugee errand, Tark and Scarlet were fighting over the TV, and Stella was rehearsing her concert piece in the girls' room, Mish beckoned me into her room and shut the door.

'Lisa says you can stay here as long as you have to. I'll send Paul over to pick up your things when he gets back. And you know you're welcome here as long as you can bear it.'

'As long as you can stand having me,' I said, out of politeness, because just then I felt like living with the Kincaids forever.

'Lisa says to tell you she's sorry for calling you selfish and pig-headed and immature.'

'Good,' I muttered. 'So she should be.' I looked up and smiled weakly. 'Because I'm not immature – no way.'

Mish smiled back. After a minute she said, 'Lisa wouldn't tell me what you called her.'

I looked at the floor. 'I said she was an interfering, narrow-minded, judgemental bitch. Something like that.'

Mish drew in a breath. 'And then you stormed out of the house?'

'Yeah.'

'Bridie, darling, don't you think that might have reminded your mother of something?'

I drew circles with my toe on the shabby rug. 'Maybe that's kind of what she said to her mum when ... when she left Brisbane?'

'Mmm, maybe.'

I rubbed my nose. 'I didn't think of that.'

'Okay.' Mish patted my knee. 'It probably won't hurt you two to give each other a bit of space, let yourselves breathe. It's not easy for Lisa, you know, to see you growing up, growing away from her. You've always been such a tight little unit, the pair of you.'

I hadn't really thought of that, either.

'And what about this church group? Are you going back, or not?'

I wrinkled up my nose. 'I'm not sure,' I admitted. 'I think I need to go back, at least one more time, to see how I feel.'

Besides, I felt like I owed it to Jay to speak to him face to face. And if Elliot *happened* to be still hanging around— I didn't let myself finish the thought.

'Wednesday, isn't it?' said Mish. 'I'll drive you.'

'*Bridie*!'

Jay rushed up and crushed me into a hug that lasted about half a minute too long. I extracted myself and he studied my face solemnly. 'How *are* you? Where have you been? I've been calling, but you never pick up. Did you lose your phone?'

'My phone …' I almost said, *my phone is busted*, but I swallowed down the lie.

'Are you okay? Chelsea said you were sick. I was worried!' He shook my shoulders, half playfully, but there was an accusing light in his eye.

My gaze slid away from his. I'd come to youth group tonight, maybe for the last time, specifically to explain myself. But a public cross-examination wasn't what I had in mind. I pulled him into a corner, and stretched the truth a little. 'I had a fight with Mum; I was feeling a bit down. Not really in the mood for church.'

'But it's when things go wrong that you need Jesus the most,' said Jay earnestly. 'And your friends, your whole community. To *lift* you into joy.'

'I just felt like being sad,' I said.

'Being negative's a waste of time,' said Jay. 'We've got so much to thank the Lord for.'

'I guess,' I said helplessly.

'Anyway, you're back.' Jay squeezed my hand. 'That's all that matters.'

'Actually, Jay, I have to talk to you about that.' I took a deep breath. 'The thing is, I've been thinking, and I'm not sure … I'm not sure I can really believe everything that you believe. I'm not sure all this is right for me.'

Jay's green-gold eye fixed itself on me, surprised and sorrowful. 'You can't give in to doubt, Bridie. That's letting the devil in.'

'See – *the devil*, that's the kind of thing I mean. I don't think I can believe in *the devil*.'

Jay looked shocked. There was a silence, then he asked abruptly, 'Is this anything to do with Elliot?'

'Elliot?' I echoed.

'He's not here. He's quit youth leadership.'

'Yes, he told me.'

'Did he?' Jay was so startled he dropped my hand.

'He just, you know, mentioned it in passing.'

'When was this?'

I know it was stupid, but Jay glaring at me, with the eye-patch and everything, made me feel as if I was being interrogated by the SS. All he needed were the jackboots and the leather cap.

'Um, on Saturday?' It seemed like years ago.

'He talked to *you* about it,' said Jay, half to himself. 'He talked to you and then ... It was Saturday night he told Dad. What did he say exactly? What did *you* say?'

'I can't remember,' I said. 'And I don't want to talk about it. It was a private conversation.'

'Okay,' said Jay slowly. 'I see.' There was a pause. I knew everyone in the room was listening, though they were pretending to ignore us. I felt hot and angry.

Jay shook his head. 'I'm not giving up on you, Bridie. You could be an amazing witness for Jesus. If you'd just trust Him, if you'd let Him right into your life, if you stopped pushing Him away ...'

'Jesus isn't a stalker, Jay!' I said, too loudly. Every head in the room swung round; no one was pretending to ignore us now.

Ryan came barging over. 'Hey, hey, hey! Let's all take a moment here.' Ryan put one hand on my shoulder and one on Jay's, simultaneously connecting and separating us. 'Simmer down, everybody. Gather round. Let's ask our Lord for some input here.' Ryan flung back his head and addressed the ceiling. 'Lord, we ask for your special help for our beloved friends Bridie and Elliot. We ask you to drive out Satan from them, to drive out their negativity and their bad energy. We ask you to forgive their doubts and questions. We ask you to restore their faith and gather them back into the embrace of your love.'

I don't know if I've ever been so embarrassed, and indignant, too. As if asking questions was *wrong* – as if daring to feel doubt about something was a *sin*! If Ryan hadn't been gripping my shoulder so hard, I would have wriggled away. I'm sure he could feel me squirming; that's probably why he squeezed so tight. My face was bright red. As soon as the prayer was over, I escaped to the other side of the room. Jay tried to follow me, but somehow I managed to evade him for the rest of the meeting. All evening, his stare pierced me, pleading and reproachful.

'You need a lift?' Chelsea asked at the end of the night.

'No, thanks.' I knew Mish was outside. I couldn't wait to run out and scramble into the safety of her car; I was almost scared someone would jump in after me, that they wouldn't let me go.

We hadn't even pulled out of the carpark when my phone began to buzz. It was Jay. I switched it off without looking at the message.

For the next few days, while I was with the Kincaids, I did something I would have thought was impossible: I left my phone turned off. I checked it at the end of every day: there were always missed calls and texts from Jay, and from school people too, which meant most mornings I had to put up with *Didn't you get …*

Jay had said he wouldn't give up on me, and he meant it. He sent a deluge of calls and messages; no doubt there was also a stack of messages piling up at home. I thanked God I wasn't there; sooner or later he'd probably turn up on the doorstep. It creeped me out a bit, but a tiny part of me felt flattered, too.

I felt safe with the Kincaids – staying with them was like taking a holiday from the rest of my life. I loved walking Tim with Stella again; I loved teasing Tark and doing the dishes with Scarlet; I loved meditating with Mish and joking around with Paul. I loved it, but it wasn't home.

Mish must have worded Stella up not to talk to me about Northside or God or anything; she didn't mention it once. I didn't think Stella had it in her to be so restrained. But then, she had to be restrained at school, too; she was still on probation. 'But I haven't felt like stirring lately,' she admitted. 'Just want to keep my head down, you know?'

That was the closest she came to saying she'd missed me.

Mum didn't ring. I knew she wouldn't; I knew she'd wait for me to make the first move. I knew it, but it still hurt. One afternoon after school, I went home to pick up some clothes. As soon as I pushed open the door, I heard Mum's voice from the living room.

'Bridie?'

I froze. Mum was *never* home at this time of day. I glanced down the hallway and caught a glimpse of her rising out of an armchair. She looked dishevelled, and she had a *cigarette* in her hand. Mum didn't even smoke! It was so unlike her that I was unnerved. I retreated, yanking my key from the lock, and fled down the street. Mum didn't follow; she didn't even call out after me.

That night Stella and Scarlet and I heard Paul and Mish muttering about it on the other side of the bedroom wall. Paul

119

thought Mum was weird, acting so detached. Mish murmured, 'That's just Lisa. She's always been hands-off.'

'Hands off?' rumbled Paul. 'Well, I'm not hands-off.'

'No, you're not,' Mish giggled, and Paul growled.

Scarlet hid her head under the blankets. 'Eew! Make them stop!'

Stella thumped the wall. 'You're *disgusting*!' she yelled. Mish and Paul fell abruptly silent, then we heard stifled laughter.

'Gross,' muttered Scarlet, rolling over.

I wriggled deeper into my sleeping-bag. A few minutes later Stella whispered, 'Bridie?'

'Mm?' I was nearly asleep.

'Not that I want you to go home or anything, but … are you ever going to talk to your mum again?'

My eyes flicked open in the dark. 'Yeah, I guess. One day.' The teenage half of me really wanted Mum, for once, to be the one who cracked first, but the kid half just wanted to run into her arms and bawl like a baby. So far the teenage half was winning, but the kid half was getting stronger.

'I was thinking …' Stella's voice was uncharacteristically tentative, 'that evolution forum's this week, the one where Lisa's speaking? I thought we could go, maybe. And you know, if you felt like it, you could say hi. And if you didn't, well, we could just … It should be interesting, Randall Martinez is speaking too.'

I was silent for a minute, then I said, 'Yeah, okay.'

'Oh, good!' Stella's voice in the darkness was breathless with relief. There was another pause, then she said softly, 'Bridie?

It's so cool to have you back. I mean, I really thought I'd lost you, you know? With all the Christian stuff ... Bridie? Are you asleep?'

I didn't say anything, and then I heard her roll over and snuggle down, and soon her breathing was as deep and regular as Scarlet's. But I lay awake for ages, staring into the dark.

I remembered what Mum had said about having to choose sides. Well, I'd made my choice: I'd chosen Stella, and turned my back on Northside. Every time Jay's number flashed up on my phone, he nudged me further away. The weeks I'd spent hanging out at youth group already felt like a bizarre aberration, as if I'd been possessed or something. That wasn't me; *this* was me: the Bridie who joked with Stella and didn't wince when she exclaimed *Jesus*! So it was over; life was back to normal.

Since I'd come to the Kincaids, I hadn't tried to pray. For a second I contemplated crawling out of my sleeping-bag and kneeling on the floor of Stella and Scarlet's bedroom. But what would I say: thanks for only killing twenty people in the war today? Thanks for sending Jay to harass me? Please God, make my mum ring me and say she's *really* sorry? Of course, I was grateful to be friends with Stella again, but I could just imagine how she'd feel if I tried to make out that was God's doing.

I didn't want to lose God. I missed that warm, protective shield, that sense that someone was watching over me. How weird that the world seemed so much emptier now than before all this started. Suddenly a universe without God seemed a cold and brutal place. *Please, God, let me believe in You again. Please come back to me.*

Just then my phone buzzed. I must have forgotten to switch it off. Still in my sleeping-bag, I caterpillared over to the desk and grabbed it. A message had come through: *Bridie? U awake? Elliot.*

I stared at it for a long moment until the light on the screen died.

'Bridie?' A sleepy mumble from Stella's bed. 'What are you doing?'

'Nothing,' I whispered. 'It's okay.' I wriggled myself back onto my mattress and curled up with the phone under my chin.

It took me a long time to fall asleep.

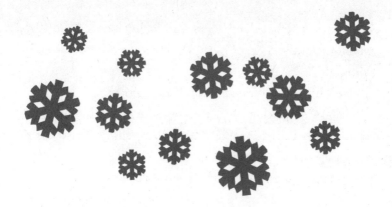

ON THURSDAY NIGHT, Stella and I arrived at the lecture theatre an hour before the forum was due to start. Protesters were already gathering outside, about fifty people shouldering placards and casually chatting. They were mostly young and swathed in scarves and overcoats. I didn't see any monkey suits. A splinter group was singing *Free to Be Yours*, a song I recognised from Northside services. I recognised a couple of faces from Northside, too: Chelsea was there, and Adam. I was scared to look too hard, in case I saw Jay. I really, really didn't want to see Jay.

Someone yelled, 'Equal time for intelligent design in schools!'

'Then get an equal argument, moron!' Stella yelled back.

Restrained Stella had disappeared for the night, apparently. I lowered my head. The Northside gang hadn't spotted me yet, but they would. 'Let's just go in,' I begged.

Stella shrugged me off. 'Can't we stay out here and bait them for a while?' Then her face changed. 'There's your boyfriend.'

My head whipped round before I could stop it. There was

Jay, between Oliver and Ryan. He hadn't noticed me – he wouldn't, unless I went over. He couldn't see very well in twilight.

'He's not my boyfriend,' I said. 'You know that.'

Stella was watching me; I knew what she was waiting to hear. I took a deep breath. 'I'm finished with Northside. I'm not going back.' As soon as I'd said it, I felt awful, like Peter pretending he didn't know who Jesus was.

Stella's face split into a huge smile. 'Yay!' She squeezed my arm, then her smile vanished. 'Look out, he's coming.'

One of the others must have spotted me. Jay weaved over to us, squinting. His face didn't light up until he was right in front of us. His eyesight must have been getting worse.

'Bridie! I knew you'd change your mind!'

I swallowed. 'Oh … no. No, I've come to hear my mum speak.'

'But you can come out afterwards. Everyone's going to be here.'

'I don't think so,' Stella butted in. 'She doesn't want anything to do with you. Get it?'

'Hang on,' I began.

Jay's face was soft with hurt and sadness. 'Is that why you haven't answered any of my messages?' he said quietly.

'I – I was going to …' I stammered.

Stella put her hands on her hips. 'I'd say if she hasn't replied to your messages, it's because she doesn't want to. It ain't rocket science.'

'Wait a minute.' I put my hand on her arm. Stella was back

in her familiar role of speaking on my behalf, and clearly loving it. The only problem was, I didn't want her to do it any more.

Suddenly I realised: it wasn't a choice between God and no God, between Northside and science, between Stella and Jay. It wasn't about finding a person, or a set of rules, to follow; it was about working it out for myself.

I seized Jay's hands. 'I'm sorry, Jay. It's not you; it's nothing to do with you. But I just can't be part of all this.' I gestured helplessly at the eager-faced protesters, the singers – who were now belting out a chorus of *He Made Us All* – at Ryan and Shanelle and Oliver.

'I'm not giving up on you, Bridie,' said Jay. 'I believe in you.'

'Don't!' I held his hands tightly between mine. 'Please, don't believe in me! I don't want you to.'

'You can walk away from me. But you can't walk away from Jesus. He won't let you.'

Stella prised my hands from Jay's. 'She can, and she is. Sheesh. What part of the word NO do you people not understand? Come on, we're going in.'

'Bridie?' Jay reached for my fingertips.

'I never wanted to hurt you,' I said. 'I'm so sorry.'

I don't know if he even heard; Stella was dragging me away. I saw him crane his head helplessly as he lost sight of us in the crowd, then the doors swung shut and I couldn't see him any more.

I shook Stella's hand from my arm. 'I hadn't finished.'

'Yeah, you had,' said Stella briskly. 'There's no point trying to have a rational discussion with these people. You're too nice, that's the problem.'

Jay *is too nice, that's the problem*, I thought. I was annoyed with Stella, but our newly repaired friendship was so fragile I didn't dare to risk telling her, so we lapsed into a strained silence.

The lecture theatre was almost full, humming with staff and students and very hot after the wintry chill outside. Technicians buzzed round with cables and sound equipment to record the forum for national radio. We managed to squeeze into seats toward the back. I was nervous; it was weird to be nervous at the thought of seeing my own mum.

Stella wriggled out of her coat. 'I can't wait to hear Lisa. We'll go and find her afterwards, yeah?'

'Yeah. All right.' I wondered what she'd say when she saw me; I wondered if she'd hug me. She never does hug me in public.

Stella said, 'Randall Martinez is supposed to be brilliant. He gets protesters everywhere he goes, so he must be doing something right.'

'We were protesting ourselves a couple of months ago,' I reminded her.

'Don't wreck my argument.' Stella's cheeks were flushed with heat and excitement. She'd left her beret on, hoping to be mistaken for a uni student. 'Are you narky with me?'

'No.'

'Sure? You seem a bit narky.'

'I'm not.' There was a pause. I wanted to say, *Stop bossing me, you're as bad as Mum, telling me what I feel, what I should think.* But I didn't. 'Is narky a word?'

'It should be.' Stella swivelled round to survey the audience. Beneath the buzz of the audience, we could hear muffled chanting from outside the building as the protesters notched up a gear. But at seven o'clock precisely, that faint noise was completely drowned out by a roar of applause as the speakers entered. Stella stuck her fingers in her mouth and wolf-whistled.

'That's for Lisa,' she yelled in my ear. 'She looks *cool*.'

Mum walked in: Dr Lisa Vandenberg, young, cool and composed in her trim black suit. I felt a surge of pride and I clapped as hard as I could. I wondered if she could see me. Five seconds later, she'd tamed the storm of applause and cheers simply by standing silently at the podium. She carried an air of quiet authority, which became even more impressive when she began to speak.

Dr Vandenberg – it was hard to think of her as Mum – was calm and reasonable as she laid out the evidence for evolution and the elegant mechanism of natural selection. This was science, she argued, it could be tested and modified. But creation theory was simply an assertion: God made the world and everything in it, end of story. There was no way to prove or disprove it, so, scientifically speaking, it was a meaningless argument.

Everyone clapped fervently as Mum sat down. Stella whispered, 'Isn't she *great*? Let's see Professor Martinez top that!'

Randall Martinez was a visiting English academic, a tubby balding little figure in a checked jacket, not impressive-looking at all. But once he stepped forward to speak, he was transformed. I couldn't tear my eyes from him. His voice was deep and compelling – a bit like Pastor Matt's, come to think of it.

'Anyone who believes in creationism is an idiot,' he declared, and a wave of warm supportive laughter rolled through the audience. Up on the platform, Mum was smiling; Stella laughed, sitting forward eagerly, her eyes bright.

'I'm not saying there is no God.' Professor Martinez strode up and down. 'I can't prove whether there is or isn't a supernatural being out there – no one can. But I think it's *very unlikely*. A supernatural being who cares what food I eat, or what I do in the privacy of my own bedroom? Please! Are you serious? So, God exists, and what's more, you can read his mind? And this all-powerful, all-knowing entity actually frets about the petty details of our everyday lives? *Really?*'

Stella was laughing; everyone was laughing. Everyone except me.

'Religious faith, belief in God, has brought humanity nothing but harm. Look at this current war – two ideas of God battling it out over the bodies of young people. It's obscene! There may have been a stage in the development of the human species when it was necessary to invent supernatural explanations for the baffling phenomena we observed, for the stars and the weather, for birth and death and sickness. I can accept that. But that time is *past*. We have science now; we can discover the *truth*. And that truth is more complicated and more wonderful than any story about the Gods!'

Mum was nodding vigorously.

'We like to think we've outgrown superstition and belief in magic. Let me tell you, religion is just another brand of mumbojumbo. It's exactly the same as believing in witchcraft! *We don't need religion.* Some people argue that religion has inspired great art, acts of courage and selflessness, the abolition of slavery and so on. Some argue that without God, there is no morality, no idea of right and wrong. But you don't need *God* to make great art or great music! You don't need *God* to tell you slavery is wrong, or murder is wrong, or torture is wrong!'

Professor Martinez paused and gazed up into the audience, directly into my eyes. His voice rose. 'But you *do* need God to justify hatred and fear – of women, of other tribes, of other ethnicities. You *do* need God to inspire war and terrorism and slavery and slaughter!'

His fist thumped on the podium and a roar of applause erupted. The audience stamped and cheered. Stella whistled. My head was spinning. I tugged at Stella's sleeve. 'I need some fresh air,' I yelled in her ear. 'Back in a minute.'

Stella stared at me. *You okay?* she mouthed.

I nodded, and Stella twisted back to Professor Martinez, who was just getting revved up. I pushed past bags and knees and coats and stumbled up the steps to the back exit. A few other people were leaving too, so I wasn't the only one who felt uncomfortable at the professor's certainties.

Behind me, a muffled explosion of laughter rocked the

theatre. I leaned against the white wall of the corridor and gulped the cool air.

'Bridie?'

My head snapped round. And there was Elliot.

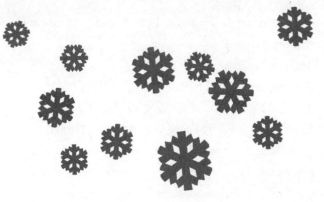

HE WAS WALKING down the corridor toward me. He'd shaved his beard off, which made him look much younger; he looked about the same age as me. He was grinning, and I realised a dumb smile was spreading over my face too.

'It was really hot in there,' I said.

He nodded. 'I had to get out. Want to take a walk outside?'

'Um, sure.' We fell into step, heading for the back of the building, away from the noise of the protesters. Elliot pushed open a heavy glass door and we emerged into a quiet courtyard. I didn't know this part of the uni at all; Mum's department was at the other end of the campus. But if I ended up studying here, I guessed a lot of my classes would be in this old building.

Elliot and I walked silently through the darkened cloisters and out onto a wide expanse of lawn outside the library. Elliot found a bench and I sat beside him.

'So you were in there too, listening?'

'Yeah,' said Elliot. 'Your mum spoke well.'

'Yeah. She was good.'

Elliot nodded. 'I wanted to hear Randall Martinez. He's got quite a reputation.'

'He's an amazing speaker.'

'He's smart, all right. Funny, too.'

'But ...' I said,

Elliot swung round to gaze intently at me. Even in the almost-dark, the searchlights of his eyes burned into me. 'But?'

I screwed my face up; I wanted to get this right. 'I couldn't exactly disagree with anything he said, but it was as though he was ignoring a whole dimension of human existence. I just can't see how, if there really is no God, if there's *nothing*, so many people all through history, in every culture, have a sense of ...'

'A presence?'

'Yes. The spiritual or the sacred. It's real, it feels real.'

Elliot stared up at the night sky. Here at the edge of the city, there was so much light that hardly any stars were visible, just a murky blanket of dark. 'Millions of people, all through history, in every culture, have believed in sorcery, too. And that the world was flat. Just because lots of people believe something doesn't make it true.'

'No, I get that. But doesn't it seem, I dunno, slightly hypo-critical to condemn all religious people for being fanatics, when he's just as rigid and intolerant about atheism being right?'

Elliot laughed softly. 'I came to hear Martinez because I wanted him to convince me. But I think he's pushed me the other way. I don't know what I believe any more. I do know that a lot of *unintelligent* people believe in God. Trust me, I've met them. But it's just not true to say that everyone who believes in God is stupid. There are plenty of wise, thoughtful, intelligent people who are religious, not just Christians. And if there *is* a God, he's everyone's God, right? There are plenty of people in the world who have had an experience of something bigger, something beyond humanity.'

'And I'm not going to throw that away just because some smart-arse, patronising, *smug* professor tells me to,' I said, with a vehemence that surprised me.

Elliot stretched his legs. 'It's funny, isn't it? Martinez talks about how arrogant the early believers were, thinking the earth was the centre of the universe. But isn't it just as arrogant to assume that human consciousness is the centre of the universe, that that's all there is?'

'Science can explain a lot, but it can't explain everything.'

'I'm not sure I *want* science to explain away courage and music, and imagination and poetry and sacrifice and joy … and love,' Elliot said.

Was he looking at me? 'I'm not sure I want to boil everything down to – to random chemicals.'

'There's got to be more to being human.'

'Maybe he's wrong, maybe human beings do need religion,' I said. 'When I think back to my life before I believed in God, it seems sort of empty, and pointless, and shallow.' My voice faltered. So I did still believe in God, did I? Maybe Jay was right: He wouldn't let me go. After a second I went on, 'I mean, I understand what he said about morality, I know we can work out that killing and hurting is wrong without needing a God to spell it out for us.'

'And a sense of wonder.' Elliot gestured up to the sky, to the stars. 'He's right; you can get that from looking through a telescope, or down a microscope.'

'But what does it *mean*?' I cried. 'What's the *point*?'

Elliot didn't reply, and we sat there in silence for a moment, looking up at the night, at all the hidden, infinite stars.

'God won't tell you what it all means, Bridie,' Elliot said at last. 'Nor what it's all for. You have to work that out for yourself. God is ... God is like a poem. God just *is*.'

'God is a poem,' I murmured. 'I like that.'

Elliot sighed and tucked his legs underneath the bench, so he was leaning forward, his hands shoved in his pockets, his breath a stream of mist. 'God is the Light,' he said. 'That's what the Quakers say. Have you heard of the Quakers?'

I shook my head.

'The Society of Friends is their proper name. Sounds good, doesn't it? They believe the Light of God is inside every person, so all people should be treated equally, and with respect. They don't have priests, or preachers, not formally. At their meetings, everyone sits in silence until someone feels moved to speak.'

'No singing and dancing?'

'I don't think so.'

'Are you going to join these Quaker people?'

He looked away. 'It's not that simple for me, Bridie. Northside is my family, my friends, my home, my whole life. Walking away from all that ...' He fell silent.

I couldn't think of anything to say. It was so much easier for me.

'Jay's out the front with the others, shouting *Martinez burn in hell*,' Elliot said abruptly.

'I know. I saw him.'

'I thought you were planning to be there, too?'

'That's not what I want from my God,' I said hesitantly.

'No,' said Elliot. 'I want a God that opens things out, not narrows them down. Do you know what I mean?'

He turned his scowly-face on me, the first time I'd seen the scowly-face in weeks. It was like a glimpse of the real Elliot, not the bland mask he'd worn at church. I felt a sting of happiness that he'd let me see it.

'*Yes*,' I said. '*That's* what God means to me. That's exactly it. God means there's more to the world, more to my life. He makes everything richer, and more meaningful – not smaller, not *less*.'

'Yes,' said Elliot. 'But sometimes it seems like the more we talk about God, the smaller He gets.'

'Is that why you like the Quakers? For the silence?'

Elliot snorted. 'Yeah, maybe.'

A silence of our own grew up between us – a comfortable, textured silence. I could have sat there forever, in spite of the cold and the dark. Elliot knew so much more than I did; he'd read more, thought more, talked to more people, explored so much further than I had. But it didn't seem to matter. It felt like we were equals. I felt closer to God in that silence with Elliot than I had for a long time. It was as if the clouds of our breath wreathed around a presence hidden in the dark and made it visible.

Elliot jiggled his knees in the cold. 'Have you thought about what course you're going to do?'

'I guess Arts. Maybe English.'

'You could try Philosophy.' Suddenly he stood up and looked down at me from his great height, hands thrust deep in his pockets. 'We'd better go back.'

I stood up too. 'Stella's still inside. We're supposed to meet Mum, afterwards.'

'It was good talking to you, Bridie. I wish—'

'I'm sorry,' I said suddenly. 'I didn't answer your message the other night.'

He frowned, as if he'd forgotten all about it. 'Oh, that's okay.'

'Let me know how you go with the Quakers.'

'Yeah.' He looked back toward the building. '*If*—' Abruptly, he began to stride back the way we'd come. I had to trot to keep up. Security guards were blocking all the doors now, so we doubled back through the cloisters and around to the front of the building. The noise of jeers and shouting grew steadily louder; the crowd of protesters weren't chatting happily any more. Their faces were distorted as they yelled their chants and jabbed their placards in the air, pushing against the line of security guards.

Elliot stopped and swore under his breath: the first time I'd heard a Northsider swear. My heart was pounding.

'There's Jay,' Elliot said, and in the same instant Jay's eye met mine. He looked from Elliot to me and back again. I felt like yelling out, *It's not what you think*. But perhaps it was.

Jay forced his way out of the crowd to where we stood. He was panting for breath, his eye-patch askew. 'This is awful,' he gasped. 'I didn't think it'd be like this.'

'What did you think it would be like?' said Elliot grimly.

The mob was howling, *We want Martinez! We want Martinez!* It was scary, an animal sound. There was a sudden roar as the double doors swung open and the protesters surged forward. I just caught a glimpse of Mum, with Stella behind her, as the security line bulged, then broke, and the crowd stampeded. I screamed, and ran blindly forward. But Elliot was beside me, and he was quicker.

'Mum! Mum!' I shrieked, but I couldn't hear my own voice. Jay was grabbing at my coat; people were pushing and shoving in all directions. I wrenched out of Jay's grip and butted through the crowd to Mum. She was on the ground, a dazed expression on her face, touching her fingertips to her head and staring at the blood. Elliot knelt beside her. He asked her something but she didn't seem to hear.

I hurled myself down on the concrete and flung my arms around her.

'Bridie, I'm okay. It's okay, Bridie.' Even now, Mum wouldn't admit she needed help. She struggled feebly to get up, but I wouldn't let her, and at last she subsided against me and let me squeeze my arms around her.

Jay was squatting beside me, saying something about Elliot. It took me a few moments to understand that he'd gone to find a taxi for us. Between us, we helped Mum stand up and she swayed against us.

Then suddenly Stella was there, her pale hair all over her face, her eyes wild, her skin blotched.

'Where the hell did you go?' she screamed at me. 'Where the hell were you?'

I gaped at her. 'I told you I was going outside.'

'Went out to join your little friends, did you? You're still one of them, aren't you?' She glared at Jay. 'Well, are you happy now? Look what you've done!'

'It wasn't Jay's fault,' I cried. 'It was an accident!'

'Some accident! They tried to *kill* us!'

'What, with chanting? Are you *crazy*?'

'Girls,' said Mum faintly, pressing her hand to the cut on her forehead. 'Girls, please.'

Elliot was at my elbow. 'I've got a taxi. This way.'

'Get lost!' screamed Stella. 'You and your mental brother and your mates, this is all your fault!'

'Shut up, you insane *bigot*!' I shouted at her.

'You're hysterical,' said Elliot to Stella, or maybe to both of us. 'You're probably in shock. This way, Lisa.'

He took Mum's arm and steered her firmly through the crowd, with me and Stella still screaming at each other, and Jay, who seemed mute with shock, trailing behind. Outside the university gate a taxi was waiting. Elliot bundled Mum and me and Stella into the back seat. As we drove off, I saw him put his arm across Jay's shoulders, and they turned away.

It was only then that I thought to wind down the window

and yell out, 'Thank you!' But I don't know if they heard me.

I slumped back in my seat, my legs like jelly. Mum fumbled for my hand. 'Bridie? Are you ... coming home?'

I nodded; my eyes were spilling with tears. Stella was still glaring at me with venom in her pale blue eyes.

'Stella, we'll drop you at home,' said Mum, organising again; she was recovering already.

'I can walk from your place,' said Stella stiffly.

'Don't be silly,' said Mum. 'It's on our way.'

'I can pick up my stuff,' I said. 'My schoolbag.'

Stella and I looked at each other across the taxi. A pulse throbbed in my neck. 'Okay,' Stella said coldly.


The three of us sat silently in the taxi while the driver told us about his rotten night, how he'd driven all the way to Werribee and not been paid. When we arrived at Stella's, she said, 'Thanks, Lisa,' and scrambled out of the door without looking at me. I unclicked my belt and followed her.

'I'll be two secs,' I told Mum.

But before I was fully out of the taxi, I could see something was wrong. The front door was open, spilling yellow light down the steps, and Mish was waiting at the gate, in a thin cardigan and yoga pants, her arms wrapped around herself.

'Mum?' Stella's voice rose in panic. 'Mum?'

'Darling.' Mish held out her hands. 'It's your nana, she's ... she's had a heart attack.'

Stella's face was white. 'Is she okay?'

'She died, Stella-bear. She's dead.'

Stella stumbled into her mother's arms. Mish caught her and led her up the steps.

They forgot to shut the door. I hesitated on the porch; the taxi was still running. I could hear Tark crying, and right down at the back of the big room Scarlet scooped up Tim and hid her face against his squirming body. I couldn't see Paul; maybe he wasn't there. Maybe he was with Nana Kincaid, wherever she was – her house, hospital?

She couldn't be dead. How could she be dead?

'Bridie?' called Mum from the taxi. 'What's happening?'

I held up my hand to her and then I darted inside and into the girls' room. My mattress was still laid out on the floor, ready for me. When I saw it, a lump rose in my throat. I grabbed my clothes from the back of the chair, my books, my school shoes, and shoved them in my pack. Then I tiptoed to the front door, seized the handle, and softly pulled it closed behind me.

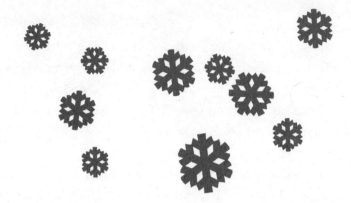

THE FUNERAL WAS on Thursday, at St John of the Cross.

It was my first funeral. I guess I'd been pretty lucky to make it to sixteen without knowing anyone who'd died.

I didn't expect Mum to come. 'You know it's in a church?' I said.

Mum frowned into the mirror as she adjusted her earrings. 'I don't give a damn whether it's in a church or not. I'm coming for Nora and for Paul and Mish and the kids. This is not about me.' She looked me up and down. 'You look very nice.'

I was wearing the skirt and shirt that I'd worn the first time Stella and I went to Northside: nice clothes, for Nana.

Nana Kincaid was the closest thing to a grandmother in my life, not counting my Brisbane gran, for obvious reasons. Nana Kincaid was often at Stella's, and always there for birthdays and parties. Sometimes, when we were younger, Stella and I went to her house after school and pigged out on bikkies. She always remembered to ask me about school, and how Mum was.

She was only eighty. That's not very old, these days. She'd

had a massive heart attack. Paul had rung her and got no answer, so he went round to her house and found her lying in bed as if she were still asleep. Was it better to die like that, without knowing anything about it, or to be sick for a while first, so you could say goodbye to people and be prepared? Prepared for what? Heaven? Hell? Or nothing?

The church was full of people in dark clothes, rustling and murmuring under the drone of the organ. I recognised lots of Kincaid faces from family gatherings. I felt sick in the stomach. A mist of sadness smothered the whole church.

At Northside, the atmosphere had been like helium, tugging everyone up, up and away into a frenzy of excitement. I wondered what a funeral at Northside would be like. I'd never seen Pastor Matt do sad; he didn't believe in dwelling on negative emotions. He'd probably say that we shouldn't be sad when someone dies, because they'd gone to be with God, and we should rejoice for them.

Rejoice? Nana was gone; how could anything fill the aching emptiness where she used to be?

The organ music changed and all Nana's family shuffled down the aisle to the front pews. Stella and Scarlet were holding hands, their fair heads bent, and Mish's arm was around Tark. Paul helped to carry in the coffin. His face was set in a grimace, and I realised he was trying not to break down.

'On the day of her baptism, our sister Nora was clothed in Christ and given the flame of faith. May Christ now welcome her to the throne of grace.'

The mysterious words rolled through the church, and the congregation murmured their replies.

'Faithful God, you have lovingly brought Nora's journey to an end. As we grieve her death we live in the hope that death opens out into glory. Amen.'

Gone into glory, gone into grace. I thought of Nana, looking out at the world through those shrewd blue eyes; eating, breathing, thinking, smiling. Now she lay inside that polished box. I swallowed hard.

'The Lord is kind and merciful …'

This was it. This was what it was all about: death. I was scared of dying. I couldn't get my mind around the fact that one day I would just stop existing. I wanted to believe that my spirit would go on, somehow – in heaven, or somewhere.

Angels, tooth fairy, Easter bunny, God.

'As for a man, his days are like grass; he flowers like the flower of the field; the wind blows and he is gone.'

I thought about all the soldiers and the young men and the children killed in the war. For every death, a family struck with grief; for every death, a crowd of people mourning. Behind every cold number, a *person* who'd laughed and danced and felt afraid, who'd argued and cuddled and sang.

Tears trickled down my face. Mum reached out and squeezed my hand, and I held it tight. One day it would be Mum up there inside the coffin; one day it would be me. But it didn't seem real; that could never happen to us.

I could feel God. He was here in the church, but I couldn't see Him. He was speaking to me, but I couldn't understand what He said. The words of the service washed over me like beautiful poetry, incomprehensible, infinitely sad, mysteriously comforting.

*God is a poem*, Elliot had said. I felt the poetry of the ancient ritual, the solemn weight of words. Maybe this was where God lived, in the words, in the acts of ritual that humans created. Maybe the very act of reaching out let us touch the mystery we reached out for.

'I am the resurrection and the life, says the Lord. If anyone believes in me, even though he dies, he will live. Anyone who lives and believes in me will not die. Alleluia.'

I felt my hand clasped in Mum's, the comfort of warm flesh. And underneath, the cold, hard bones.

'Give her eternal rest, O Lord, and may your light shine on her forever.'

'Amen,' I whispered, and then I heard Mum whisper, 'Amen.'


Afterwards, the congregation milled around outside the church talking, as if it was a weird, subdued, old people's party.

Mum checked her watch. 'I'll have to leave for work soon. Do you want to go to school or back to the Kincaids' for the wake?'

'The what?'

'After they take the body to be buried.' *The body*. Not Nana, not Nora, not Mrs Kincaid. Not a person any more, just a body, just a husk. 'After the burial, everyone will go back to Mish and Paul's for a drink and something to eat.'

'I don't think Stella will want me,' I said bitterly.

Mum's memory of the forum night was hazy. She didn't

remember Stella and me screaming at each other; she didn't believe it had really happened. She nudged me in Stella's direction. 'Go and ask her. I think she'd like you there.'

'I think you're wrong.'

'You won't know till you do the experiment. Go on.'

I shrugged and edged toward Stella. She was standing by herself, over to one side of the doors. She was paler than usual, but she wasn't crying. Paul had cried the whole time; I'd heard him steadily weeping through the service, and he was still blinking through tears now, even as he shook hands and hugged and smiled at people.

'Hi,' I said awkwardly.

Stella looked away. 'Thanks for coming.'

'It was kind of beautiful.'

'You think?'

'I think Nana would have—'

'Loved it?' Stella turned her cold pale blue gaze on me.

'So many people ...' I faltered. 'Everyone loved her ...'

'You think it's worth *dying* to see how many people loved you?'

'No, of course not.'

'It's all right for you.' Stella's face twisted. 'I suppose you think Nana's up there in a white nightie, playing a harp. But she's *not*. She's nowhere. She's gone.' Stella began to cry, tears slipping down her cheeks. 'I want my Nana back.'

Mish hurried over and put her arm around Stella, and Stella leaned into her and sobbed. 'Come on, honey,' Mish murmured. 'It's time.'

I backed away. 'Mum has to go …'

'Thank you both for coming,' said Mish. 'Tell Lisa we really appreciate it.'

I muttered something incoherent as Mish led Stella away, then I ran back to Mum. 'Drop me at school.'

Mum looked at me. 'Give Stella time. She's upset.'

'Yeah,' I said. It was as if Stella blamed me for Nana dying, as if all the Christians had got together and snatched her grandmother away.

Mum fumbled in her bag. 'God, I'd kill for a cigarette.'

'*Mum*!'

'Churches make me jittery.'

'I thought it was sort of beautiful.'

Mum shot me a look. 'Yes,' she admitted. 'Me too.'

The Catholic church seemed to have a weight to it, a solemnity that Northside lacked. All that tradition, I guess. And it had a poetry, too, that Northside definitely didn't have. Maybe I could be a Catholic …

But there was all that stuff Stella and Nana had argued about: the virgin birth and trans-whatever it was, and heaven and hell, and sin and confession. I wasn't sure if I could make myself believe in all that, or that I could belong to a church that didn't treat women as whole human beings.

Didn't God have any house where I could feel at home?

We walked toward our car as the hearse, heaped with flowers, glided past. Mum said, 'It's funny how people cling to the old rituals. Paul was adamant that he wanted a traditional Mass for Nora, you know. I wouldn't be surprised if he wants the same for himself, when his turn comes. Funeral parlours can be so unsatisfying. When I die —'

'You're not going to die!' I cried, and hugged her tight, right in the middle of the road, and I was crying. She felt so fragile in my grasp, so much smaller than she used to be; we were the same height now. 'Nothing's going to happen to you!'

'Well, I certainly hope not.' Gently, Mum pushed me away and wiped my face with a tissue from her handbag. 'Not for a long time, anyway. Come on, Bridie, don't be silly! We'll be late.'

But it didn't feel silly. All that day I couldn't stop thinking about death, and how it descended without warning, swift as a guillotine, and how vulnerable we all are, how desperate for comfort. And I wished Mum had hugged me back, that she'd told me everything would be all right forever, because that was what I wanted to hear.

That was what the priest had tried to say, what Pastor Matt preached every Sunday: that everything would be all right, that we were loved, that we'd always be safe forever, even after we died.

Stella couldn't believe that, that was one reason why she was so angry now. And I knew Mum didn't believe it either, so she would never say it, even to comfort me. That cool, clear bravery was what made Mum strong, her ability to face reality without flinching. She'd never needed to tag along behind anyone. Without that strength, she never could have stood up to her parents; she never could have kept me. She wouldn't have survived. She would never pretend only to make me, or herself, feel better.

But just this once, I wished she'd tried.


That night after I'd gone to bed, I heard Mum creep out of her study and pick up the phone. There was a long silence, and then I heard her voice. It was muffled. She was crying.

'Hello, Mum? It's me. It's Lisa.'

There was a long pause. My eyes were wide open in the dark. Silently I prayed, *Don't let her hang up.*

And then I heard Mum say, 'Yes, good. She's in Year 11 now. Yes, I'm very proud of her.'

I rolled over and stared into the dark. *Thank you, God.* Peace wrapped around me like a cloak, and I slept.

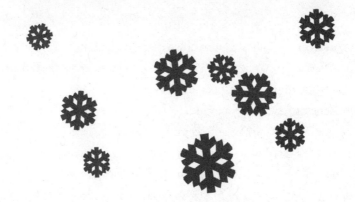

ON THE SUNDAY after Nana's funeral, I woke so early it was still dark. There was no reason to get up, I could have huddled in bed for hours but I felt completely wide-awake and restless.

Thoughts batted inside my brain like moths fluttering round a light globe. First there was Elliot. Mum and I had both tried to call him, to thank him for helping us at the forum, but his phone was switched off. That was poetic justice for me. And when Mum rang him at home, they always said he was out.

Jay had sent me one last text: *RU OK?*

I stared at it for a long time, not knowing what to say. At last I texted back, *I'm sorry.* He hadn't replied, and I was relieved. Jay and I didn't understand each other. I didn't think we ever would. After talking to Elliot, I knew I would never go back to Northside. I was looking for a God large enough to embrace scientific knowledge, not deny it; a God large enough to accept that sadness and anger and doubt were normal, not 'negative attitudes'; a God who spurred me to strive to be a better person, but who would forgive me if I failed. Northside's God was too small.

I kept thinking about what Elliot had said, about how God should open things out, not close them off, and how God was a poem. Sometimes I thought I almost understood what he meant. Since that night, and especially at Nana's funeral, a sense of the presence of God had come back to me. I could talk to Him; I could pray; I could feel His grace around me.

But I wanted more. I wanted a place to go where I could feel what I'd felt at Northside in the beginning: the joy of sharing that grace. It was okay to talk to God, all alone in my bedroom, but Northside had taught me that it was even more wonderful to celebrate His presence with a crowd of other people all feeling the same.

He, Him – Stella was right, making God male bugged me too. But calling God 'it' wasn't right either.

The thought of Stella gave me a pang. If only she wasn't so furious with me. Maybe she'd never stopped being angry. Maybe all the time I was staying at her house, her anger had been bubbling away like lava under the crust of our friendship, waiting for a reason to erupt. She couldn't forgive me. She thought I'd dumped her for God; she wouldn't be happy till I dumped God and she was the centre of my life again.

As the dawn light filtered through the window, I threw off the doona and pulled on my oldest trackies and parka. It was foggy outside, and frost glinted on the grass of the nature strip.

There was no sound from Mum's room; she was still asleep. I let myself quietly out of the front door. The street was shrouded in white mist. The world was utterly silent. I might have been the only person alive.

I didn't want to risk running into Stella. In fact, I didn't want to run into any Kincaids. So I deliberately turned away from their house, away from the highway and the river, and began to walk in the opposite direction, turning corners at random, choosing streets I didn't know, trying to lose myself in the fog. My runners were silent on the damp footpath. In my dark tracksuit pants and my dark parka, I was a shadow in the mist, a dark ghost slipping through the whiteness.

If Nana's ghost came back, she'd sit on the end of Stella's bed and say, *I told you there was life after death, Miss Smarty-Pants. Don't you roll your eyes at me!* I imagined the look on Stella's face. If only I could ask Nana if she'd seen God; she'd be able to clear it all up for me.

Everyone I knew seemed to have a different idea about what God was. According to Elliot, God was a poem; to Jay, He was a friend; to Stella, a fairytale. To Randall Martinez, God was an imaginary policeman, laying down irrational laws; to Mum, He was an unforgiving tyrant who ordered her parents to disown her. According to Ryan, God was the creator who made the world; for Paul, He was the world itself; for Mish, He was some vague spirit that could manifest anywhere.

And what about for me?

It seemed to me that God was a kind of magnet that kept pulling me toward Him even when I tried to pull away; a force that dragged my compass back and back, no matter how hard I resisted.

I clambered up the hill, away from the river. My legs ached, and I was starting to feel hungry. A main road was up ahead, lined with shops. There would be cafes open there, but I hadn't brought any money. A man in a long velvet skirt gave me a smile. Startled, I smiled back. He wandered on, vanishing into the fog, another ghost on this ghostly morning.

I crossed over the main road and through a park. A wet slide loomed against the white sky. Swings hung limp and still. There wasn't much traffic on the streets; the houses were blind and silent. The whole world was empty and sad, and the only person moving in it was me – me and the guy in the velvet skirt.

I walked for hours past Edwardian cottages and California bungalows. When Stella first decided to become an architect, we taught ourselves the names of all the house styles and she used to test me on our walks. Thinking about Stella made me sad again. I crossed a bridge over a creek, and another wide highway, and walked along random deserted streets, the fog dissolving around me.

Then I heard the music.

It was a Zita Mariposa song, one of my favourites – *Flame* – but it wasn't Zita Mariposa singing. It sounded like a group of voices, not far off. I hurried after the sound, around a corner and down a hill, and then I realised that I was almost back where I'd started, a couple of blocks from my house. And I knew where the song was coming from. It was drifting from the little ramshackle weatherboard church on the corner of Enid Street. The tiny carpark beside the church was lined with cars, and someone had parked a motorbike on the footpath. The church door was open, and the words of *Flame* wavered out into the winter morning, carried by an unsteady choir of men and women and children all singing together. It wasn't the massive soaring choir of Northside, there couldn't have been more than about twenty people singing, but there was a purity and a warmth and a gladness in the voices that held me there, listening.

I was just in time to hear the end of the song. As I hovered on the footpath, a middle-aged woman darted out to close the door. She saw me and smiled.

'Bit chilly,' she said. 'Want to come in?'

I hesitated, then shook my head. The woman smiled again and said, 'Well, if you change your mind, just push it open.' She vanished back into the church.

I sank down on the steps, suddenly exhausted. I couldn't hear the service inside, just the low murmur of voices and an occasional ripple of laughter. I leaned against the shabby weatherboards, somehow comforted to know that on the other side there were people talking to God, and thinking about Him, even if I wasn't with them.

I closed my eyes, bowed my head and buried my cold hands deep in my pockets. Gradually my tense body started to relax. I began to be aware of the sounds around me: distant traffic, the chatter of birds, the rumble of a bus, the rhythm of my own breathing, and the low, steady rise and fall of the voices inside the church. The thoughts that had been frantically chasing round my head gradually slowed down, and melted away.

New thoughts took over, still circling, but slowly now – sad thoughts about Stella, and whether we'd ever be friends again;

memories of the peace rally, when we were so full of hope, and how our hopes had drained away like blood in the streets of faraway, dusty cities. I thought about Mum, and how scared I was of losing her, but how, at the same time, I kept feeling this impulse to push her away. I thought about my grandparents, and whether I wanted to see them again. I thought about Nana Kincaid, wherever she was, and about Elliot and Jay and the mess I'd made of it all. I hoped Jay knew I hadn't meant to hurt him. Eventually, the warm, constant murmur of the service seeped through the walls of the church and folded around those thoughts and carried them away.

And then I was left with God.

I hadn't known it was possible to pray without words. That a prayer could lie in silence.

I realised I was crying. Sobs rolled up and out of my throat, tears shuddered through me. I knew I should get up and leave, that the congregation inside would hear me, but I couldn't move. I was paralysed, blinded by tears. I covered my face with my hands and let it all out, all the formless, wordless sorrow and confusion and yearning of this strange winter. The churning anger I felt toward Stella and Jay and Elliot and Mum, and God, too. Everything I'd been trying to squash down dissolved and washed away, until I was weeping – not happily, exactly, but with relieved exhaustion. I was wrung out and limp.

And then the door creaked open above me, and someone put their arm around my shoulders and led me inside. It was the woman who'd spoken to me before. I stumbled up the steps and let her sit me down on a bench at the rear of the church – not the part where the service was being held, but a kind of annexe where morning tea was laid out on a long table, and an urn for hot drinks steamed. At the front of the church, a man with a beard and glasses was reading from the Bible. Children squirmed round to peer at me over the backs of long benches.

The woman sat down beside me, still with her arm round me. She nodded in the direction of the urn and mouthed *Tea?* I smiled gratefully, groping in my pocket for a hanky. She brought me a steaming mug of hot, sweet tea and I gulped it, feeling its warmth spread through my chilled body. The man reading from the Bible shot a glance in my direction and gave me a half-smile, which I was too embarrassed to return. I stared down at my mug. I couldn't imagine what these people must think of me. But at the same time, it was so calm and peaceful and friendly that I knew it didn't matter.

'Let us pray,' said the man at the front, and with everyone else, I bowed my head. For a few moments we prayed in silence, and the circle of strangers held me safe, in a warm, breathing silence that was a kind of love.

Then the bearded man said, 'We thank you, Lord, for bringing us together in your presence to worship you today, whether we are joyful or in distress. We welcome old friends and unexpected visitors, and we pray for your blessing on us all.'

Then there was silence again. And it struck me that Elliot was half right about God being a poem. Because it seemed to me that God was somewhere else, too – in the spaces between the words, in the silences. And wherever a group of people gathered to be with Him, there He was. And I was glad to be here, with Him, and with them.

The middle-aged woman smiled at me. 'Biscuit?' she said.

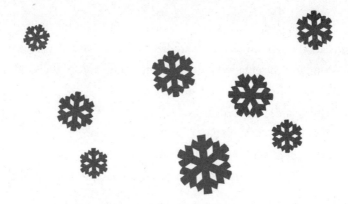

I HEARD THEM COMING long before I saw them.

Spring had officially started a week ago, but it was still freezing there on the beach, before sunrise, with the icy breeze blowing off the sea. I was warm enough inside my parka, but my face and ears tingled with cold. I hoped Mish had persuaded Stella to rug up properly. Maybe not: I could hear Stella's voice raised in complaint, as their feet thudded down the wooden steps.

'I'm *cold*. This was a dumb idea. What's wrong with walking by the river? Then we could have brought Tim. Let's go and get a coffee. I'm *freezing*.'

I stood up, hands jammed into my pockets. The morning star hung bright in the navy blue sky, and a crack of light had appeared between the dark blocks of sea and sky, wedging them apart.

Two shadowy figures were silhouetted on the walkway, one in a striped beanie, one in a parka with a furry hood. 'But look, Stella. Isn't it beautiful?' I heard Mish say.

'I guess,' said Stella grudgingly, and sent the curtain of her hair flick, flick, back over her shoulders. Then she saw me.

She stopped dead, staring, not sure in the dim light if it was really me. Mish prodded her onward, and slowly they descended the remaining steps and tramped across the sand to the clump of rocks where I stood.

'Hi,' I said.

'You knew she'd be here!' Stella said to Mish.

'Well, der,' said Mish. 'Hi, Bridie.'

'Mum's waiting in the car.' I gestured back to the top of the cliff. 'She's got coffee.'

'Ooh, good.' Mish rubbed her hands. 'See you later, girls.'

'*Mum*!' said Stella.

Mish turned back. 'Haven't you two got things to talk about?'

Stella kicked at a rock. 'This is a conspiracy. I should have *known*.'

'Oh, shut up, Stell,' I said. 'Sit down and watch the sunrise.'

I lowered myself back onto my rock, and after a minute Stella arranged herself gingerly on a rock nearby, jiggling her knees in the cold. We both stared out to sea as the waves crashed and hissed onto the sand.

The line of light along the horizon grew wider, deepening into gold, and the inky blue of the sky gradually faded, the colour receding before the sun. A dazzling spot appeared on the horizon, too bright to look at. The flecks of faraway cloud were tinted pink and gold and amethyst. It was so bright we had to shield our eyes. When we looked again, the sun was up, a ball of white fire tossed into the air and hanging there, breathing gold all over the world.

I let out a deep breath.

'Yeah, well,' said Stella. 'That was pretty nice. But it doesn't prove there's a God.'

'Jeez, Stella,' I said. 'Can't you talk about anything but God? Get over it!'

We looked at each other and burst out laughing. Then we sat in silence for a while, watching the sun rise higher, and the waves run up and back across the golden sand.

'Dad reckons we're going to get a flood of refugees from the war soon,' Stella said.

'Yeah?'

'His refugee group's looking for volunteers to teach English and stuff, help get people settled in. I said he could sign me up.' Stella gave me a sideways glance. 'Don't suppose you want to, too?'

'*Yeah*,' I said. 'I'd love to help – to do something real.'

'More useful than marching,' said Stella.

'Marching's important, too.' I hesitated, then said, 'There's this group called the Quakers, they were at the rally too. Did you see them? I've been checking them out. They're pacifists from way back. They fought for the abolition of slavery and women's rights, even back in the seventeenth century. They're really big on social justice. Greenpeace and Oxfam and Amnesty International were all started by Quakers.'

'Wow,' said Stella. 'They sound cool.'

'There's a catch,' I said.

'Oh,' said Stella. 'Don't tell me. They're Christians, right?'

'Right. Elliot told me about them.'

'*Oh*,' said Stella significantly. 'Are you going to be Quakers together?'

'I haven't seen Elliot for ages,' I said uncomfortably. 'And I haven't even been to a Quaker Meeting yet. They do sound cool, though. They're really into the whole equality thing. In the olden days they were always in trouble because they wouldn't take their hats off or bow, even to the King. And they won't swear oaths, because they think you should tell the truth all the time, not just when you swear to.'

'They sound all right,' said Stella, 'you know, for God-botherers.' She slid off her rock onto the sand and wriggled her bum into a hollow. 'You going to stay up there on the moral high ground or come down in the dirt with me?'

I slid down beside her. 'I thought you were the one on the moral high ground.'

'Me? Nuh.' Stella looked away. 'I'm just scared, that's all.'

It was a shock to hear her say it out loud. I shaded my eyes from the sun so I could see her face. 'Really?'

Stella rested her cheek on her knee. She dug her fingers into the sand and mumbled, 'I thought you'd skip off with your shiny new friends and you wouldn't need me any more.'

'If you hadn't gone to St Marg's—'

'I never wanted to go to St Marg's!'

'I know! But I'm just saying. You did go, and I missed you. I had a – an opening for some new friends, and Jay and Elliot and Northside came along.'

Stella sniffed, and wiped her nose on her sleeve. 'Yeah, well, that's a pretty lame excuse for *abandoning* me.'

'I *didn't*.'

'Well, it felt like it. Okay, maybe you didn't, but I was scared you would, all right? I thought you'd change. I thought you'd turn into a different person. I thought you'd get all stupid and judgemental and prejudiced, and only believe what other people told you to believe and never think about anything for yourself.'

'And have I turned into that person?'

Stella chucked a pebble across the sand. 'Not *yet*.'

'I think it's been the opposite. I think I've asked more questions and thought more about things this winter than I ever have in my life!'

Stella didn't say anything; she drew lines on the sand with her finger.

'Maybe some of the people at the evolution forum only believed what Randall Martinez told them to believe.'

'Maybe,' mumbled Stella.

'Anyway,' I said. 'It wasn't just about finding new friends. I was looking for something. I still am looking for something.'

'Yeah? What?'

'I dunno.' I felt embarrassed, but I made myself say it anyway. 'Grace?'

'I don't know what that means,' said Stella.

'I don't either,' I confessed. 'Not technically. But I know it when I feel it.'

'So you have found it?'

'Yeah, I think so. A couple of times.'

'What does it feel like?'

I was quiet for a moment before I answered. 'Well, I felt it when we were all singing our hearts out at Northside. And at Nana's funeral. And when I prayed with the people at the little church on the corner – I've been going there sometimes. And just now, watching the sun come up, the beauty of it all …' There was one other time: when Elliot and I had trusted each other in the half-dark with our questions, and with our uncertainties, but I couldn't share that with Stella. She wouldn't understand. So I said, 'It's being grateful – and joyous – and feeling so small, but part of something magnificent. And when other people are there, too, sharing it, it's like you bring God into the room with you, just by being together – oh, I can't explain.'

'Lucky you,' said Stella.

'You're laughing at me.'

'No, I'm not.' Stella brushed the sand off her hands. 'Listen, Bridie, we have to stop being scared of what the other's going to say. So what if we have an argument? It's not the end of the world if we think differently. You believe in God. I don't. So what? Let's fight about it. Maybe you'll change my mind. You won't *break* if I disagree with you, neither will I. *We* won't break.'

'Won't we?'

The wind whipped Stella's hair across her face. 'No, we won't,' she said quietly. 'Not now. Okay?'

'Okay,' I said.

Stella gave a shaky laugh. 'Check us out. Demanding world peace, and the two of us fall apart over … over …'

'Philosophical differences?'

'Yeah.'

'It does sound pretty lame when you put it like that,' I admitted.

Stella traced a long winding S in the sand, and I added a bulbous B beside it. Stella drew squiggles all around our initials.

'I was talking to a woman at the little church,' I said. 'And she said doubt is good. She said all faith is built on doubt. That's how you start to believe in the first place, from a little seed of doubt, and that's how you keep your faith strong, by asking the hard questions, by doubting. And that's why I need you, Stell, because you're so good at asking the hard questions. You stop me being lazy, you make me keep thinking.'

'And that's good, is it?'

'Yeah, that's good.'

'I was thinking I might come back to school next year,' said Stella, still absorbed in the patterns in the sand.

'Seriously? What do Mish and Paul say?'

'Well, they're not exactly rapt. But I've had a crap year at St Marg's. I reckon I can talk them round.'

'Cool. But even if you can't, there's always uni.'

'Yeah, there's always uni. So are you going to call Elliot? Come on, Bridie, don't be a wuss. He can take you to the Quakers. Or you could take him to your little church. Mum says she's going to become a Buddhist, you could try that. Or maybe you and Elliot could start your own church, now *that's* an idea.'

I laughed. 'Has anyone ever told you you're bossy, Stella Kincaid?'

'No, never. What *are* you talking about?'

There was a pause. 'Mum and I might be going to Brisbane this summer,' I said.

Stella's eyebrows flew up. 'To see your grandparents?'

'Yeah. Mum rang them after – after Nana's funeral. She says she's been angry for so long, and she doesn't want to be angry forever. And they're getting old. They wanted us to come for Christmas, but Mum says she's not ready for that yet, so we'll probably go in January.'

'Wow,' said Stella. 'Hardcore. How do you feel about that?'

'I'm not sure.' I was quiet for a moment. 'Mum might have stopped being angry, but I've only just started, know what I mean? I'm a bit scared. But I guess I'll go.'

'It'll be weird, for sure. But you never know, it might turn into a summer of love.'

I snorted. 'You think?'

I hoped it might be a summer of forgiveness, or a summer of understanding, or at least a summer of trying to understand – a season to follow my winter of grace.

Stella stood up and brushed her hands on her jeans. 'I'm still freezing. Want to see if Lisa and Mish have left us any coffee?'

'Those two? No way. But we could make them buy us one.'

'Hey, I'm holding out for a breakfast with the lot. I'm *starving*.' And Stella began to jog back across the sand toward the steps to the carpark.

I lingered on the beach. I'd follow Stella in a minute; because

I wanted to, not because I had to. Another thing I'd learned this winter was that I didn't have to rely on other people to tell me what to believe or do or think. I could listen to the voice inside me and decide for myself. It wasn't always easy to hear; and whether I called it God, or the Light, or my conscience, or whatever, didn't really matter. And whether I found it at Northside, or St John's, or at the little weatherboard church, or with the Quakers or the Buddhists, or all alone on the beach didn't matter either. At least now I knew how to listen.

I took one last look around the deserted sand, the sparkling sea, the wide sky marbled with streaks of rosy cloud. It was going to be a beautiful day.

# About the Author

KATE CONSTABLE was born in Melbourne. She spent some of her childhood in Papua New Guinea, without television but close to a library where she 'inhaled' stories. She studied Law at Uni before realising this was a mistake, then worked in a record company when it was still fun. She left the music industry to write the Chanters of Tremaris series: *The Singer of All Songs*, *The Waterless Sea* and *The Tenth Power*, as well as a stand-alone Tremaris novel, *The Taste of Lightning*. Kate lives in Melbourne with her husband and two daughters.